NOBLE ROT

Also by Will Harriss

Timor Mortis
The Bay Psalm Book Murder

NOBLE ROT

WILL HARRISS

ST. MARTIN'S PRESS NEW YORK

Design by Dawn Niles

Library of Congress Cataloging-in-Publication Data

Harriss, Will.
    Noble rot / Will Harriss.
    p. ; cm.
    "A Thomas Dunne book."
    ISBN 0-312-08865-5
    I. Title.
    PS3558.A673N6   1993
    813'.54—dc20   92-21218
                                                     CIP

First edition: April 1993

10 9 8 7 6 5 4 3 2 1

This is for Elizabeth, my own Point Zéro

ACKNOWLEDGMENTS

Numerous people contributed to this story, most notably two famous vintners in Napa who furnished invaluable information about wineries and wine making—and saved me from laughable blunders. They prefer to remain anonymous, but let it be said that their generosity and hospitality are equaled only by their marvelous wines. Jay Goetting—possibly the finest member the Napa County Board of Supervisors ever had—and his wife, Sherry Goetting, supplied printed, written, spoken, and photographic information about the Napa County Board. My daughter Wendy Brewer educated me about custom-tile design. Deputy Sheriffs Tom Gorman and Bill White of the Napa County Sheriff's Department were amazingly generous with their time and expertise, as was Officer Richard Burgess of the St. Helena Police Department. No author could ask for better friends.

NOBLE
ROT

ONE

A cross the blackness of the night, dawn began as a thin red razor-slash along the low mountain ridge to the east.

A puff of breeze ruffled the feathery leaves of the California peppertree overhanging the flagstone walk.

Vinnie Letessier came out of the house and sauntered down the walk to the winery's fermentation room, whistling "I'm the Most Happy Fella in the Whole Napa Valley." He truly felt that way. For the first time in his twenty-five years, someone actually needed him. Not only that, the work was interesting. Work could even be fun. He was eager to get at it—a notion that would have shocked his friends down in Los Angeles. As for getting up before dawn, that wasn't so bad. He'd never done it for *work* reasons, to be sure, but you have to rise with the lark if you want first crack at one of UCLA's tennis courts.

The rattling of his key in the lock startled a finch in the honeysuckle vines framing the door, and the bird fluttered out, beating its wings. Vinnie jumped, afraid it was a bat.

The key wouldn't turn in the lock. When he twisted it the other way—clockwise—he heard the latch bolt slide shut. That was puzzling. It meant the door was unlocked to begin with. He must have left it unlocked last night. Uncle Francis would not be happy about that if he knew, but he didn't know, and Vinnie certainly wasn't going to mention it. *Pas si bête.* Let sleeping cats lie, as the French say.

He swung the door open and flicked a switch. A silent explosion of silver light bounced from the huge stainless steel fermentation tanks that marched in a column of twos down the aisle, each giant cylinder holding almost four thousand gallons of wine. His nostrils filled again with the odd scent of damp earth and dried wine and trampled grapes.

Vinnie strolled down the aisle, stepping over hoses, around pumps, around smaller tanks of diatomaceous earth for filtering the wine, until he arrived at F17, the tank he was to rake out. This was scut work, but it made him feel like an old Napa Valley winery hand anyway, because now, after only nine or ten weeks, he could already toss off such terms as "racking off the lees" and "pumping over" and "breaking the chapeau" and "topping the ullage"—not bad for a guy with an M.A. in French (although he wasn't exactly sure what ullage was, or why it needed topping).

He opened the round manhole door at the base of F17 and peered through his black-framed glasses at the pomace inside—the thick mass of purple grape skins and seeds, mingled with dead bees, bird droppings, dirt, sulfur, pollen, feathers, and God-knows-what-all. As Uncle

Francis said once, it was lucky for winemakers that the dumb American public didn't know how filthy grapes are when they're first crushed. Now, the partly clear cabernet sauvignon in F17 had been racked off into another tank, leaving Vinnie the job of raking out the leftover crud at the bottom.

He took up a long-handled rake and pulled a mass of the stuff out through the manhole and into a tub. Easy enough so far. But when he inserted the rake again, farther in, it snagged on something—something heavy and solid, not like pomace at all. Vinnie pressed down on the rake handle and pulled hard.

A man's head slid through the hole, face up. Vinnie jumped back, slipped, dropped the rake and fell on his behind on the concrete floor. He hyperventilated for half a minute before working up the nerve to get up and take a closer look.

The face of the corpse was dyed a ghastly purple. Somehow it was even more grotesque that the hair was dyed purple too, and that the open mouth—with a glint of gold showing in the purple teeth—was clogged with grape skins.

Vinnie's own mouth opened. He backed up three steps, turned, and hurried out to rouse Uncle Francis.

TWO

Francis Letessier's face had the mixture of puffiness and alarm seen in people who are yanked out of deep sleep. He wore yesterday's soiled white shirt, crumpled trousers, bedroom slippers. The hair in his black tonsure stuck out over his ears. He stared at the dead man for a long while through his own black horn-rims. The expression on his face turned stony.

"Catastrophe. This . . . is catastrophe."

Vinnie was surprised that he spoke so quietly.

"Who is he, Uncle Francis?"

Francis ran his hand over his bald pate, tanned by the summer sun.

"*Nom de dieu de nom de dieu de nom de bon dieu!*"

His uncle rarely broke into French these days. Vinnie

supposed that the dead man must have been important to him.

"Is he a friend of yours?"

"Let's get him out of there."

Francis rolled up his sleeves and grabbed a handful of purple shirt at the corpse's left shoulder. It was a Mexican wedding shirt of the type still popular among gringos but no longer worn by Mexicans at weddings. The shirt appeared to be much too large—baggy—an XL on an S corpse. Vinnie hung back.

"Come on, come on, come on!"

Vinnie sucked in his lower lip and grabbed the other shoulder. The corpse slid out of the tank and the legs flopped limply to the floor.

"Let's hose him off," said Francis.

"Who is he? Is he one of the Mexican workers?"

Francis gave him an irritated glance. "Does he look Mexican?"

"Why do you want to hose him off?"

"Just get the hose, all right?"

"Aren't you going to notify the police?"

"That's why I want the hose."

Vinnie gaped at his uncle, who had now gone wild-eyed behind his horn-rims and had made the mistake of rubbing his hand over his bald pate again, leaving purple streaks on it.

Vinnie avoided his uncle's eyes, but looking at the corpse was no treat either. It made him feel a little cuckoo himself. For one crazy moment he thought of the dead man as coming from Gillikin country in the Land of Oz, where everybody wore purple clothes.

A hokey grin appeared on Vinnie's face.

"Uncle Francis. Are you sort of, uh, hoping to cover this up?"

"Cover what up?"

"The stiff being in the tank. Is that why you want to hose him off?"

"Well, it isn't to shampoo the son of a bitch."

"Uh huh."

Uncle and nephew looked at each other.

"Think he was murdered?" said Vinnie.

"Oh no, he was homeless so he just crawled in there for the night. Look, do I have to get that hose myself?"

"How do you think he really got in there?"

"Whoever killed him put him in."

"But why?"

"Vincent! Will you please get the goddamn hose!"

"Okay! No problem!"

Near the door Vinnie picked up a red rubber hose, twisted the nozzle shut, turned on the water, and dragged the hose down to his uncle, but when his uncle reached for it, Vinnie hesitated.

"Unk—listen—you know a hell of a lot more about wine than I do, but can I ask a question? Will water really wash all the wine off this guy?"

Instead of answering, his uncle glared at him; then, to his surprise, he saw Uncle Francis's expression melt all the way down from defiance to defeat and despair. Finally, to Vinnie's astonishment, Uncle Francis—that man of iron and acid—permitted his eyes to shimmer with tears.

"Hell, no! . . . *Merde, merde, et mille fois merde!* Put the goddamn hose back where you got it. *Cent mille troupeaux de cochons!*"

Uncle Francis gazed down at the corpse—this albatross, this curse.

"We'll dump him somewhere else."

"We?"

"It'll take two of us."

"But Unk!"

"Stop calling me Unk! You sound like you're straining your bowels. Are you going to help me or not?"

"If you don't mind, I'd rather not."

"Oh, you'd rather not, would you! There's gratitude! We face total ruin, but you'd 'rather not.' "

"Hell, Uncle Francis, I'm grateful to you!"

Francis snorted.

"Sure I am! I was in one hell of a shape, you know that. Totally *fini*. You saved my ass when all I had left in the world was an M.A. and a car. You are truly a nice guy, and don't think I don't know it. Even Ezra knows it."

"I am *not* a nice guy, damn it! I just keep getting *trapped* into doing the so-called right thing. And if you're so goddamn grateful, go get the pickup truck. And hurry up while it's still dark."

"Okay, but another question. Which would get you in worse trouble: Leaving this guy where he is, or getting caught dumping him into the Napa River?"

"What if we don't get caught?"

"There's still the wine."

"What about the wine?"

"Would you really sell the wine from that tank? Or drink it yourself?"

Francis Letessier's shoulders slumped, and he sat down on a filter tank. "Damn, damn, damn! No, you little bastard, I would not. Unless I was sure it wasn't contaminated."

Little bastard? Vinnie was a lanky 6'3. "Maybe it wasn't."

"What makes you say that?"

"Look how limp the guy is. If rigor mortis hasn't set in, maybe he was stuck in there *after* the wine was racked off into another tank."

Francis looked up with hope in his eyes.

"If you're right . . ."

"And anyway," Vinnie went on, "weren't you exaggerating just a soupçon, Uncle Francis? Could losing one tank really ruin you?"

"I've already lost a tank of cabernet franc from last year's vintage. Those two sons of bitches I fired sneaked

8

in and drained it. And this tank here, Vincent, contained close to four thousand gallons of must from my prize special reserve cabernet sauvignon. Fourteen tons of grapes—nearly a thousand cases of wine! Call it a hundred fifty thousand dollars. Maybe more."

"What about insurance?"

"My insurance lapsed. At least the important parts."

"Jesus, how come?"

"Lovely Adrienne. She and her lawyers cleaned me out of cash—two hundred thirty-three thousand dollars and eighty cents, to be exact—and I'm supposed to give her five thousand a month alimony until she marries again. I already had a big loan from the bank and I borrowed more. I had a payroll to meet. I had to buy three hundred *Limousin* oak barrels at two hundred eighty-five dollars apiece. And now, if the news gets out there's been a dead body in my wine, just how much Château Letessier do you think I'm going to sell?"

"It's that bad?"

Francis shrugged his shoulders, threw up his hands, and turned away from the body on the floor.

"Well, let's see what we can salvage out of this mess. Go notify the police in St. Helena. The Chief and I have always been friendly. And try to get back before the crew shows up."

"Why not phone?"

"There's always reporters hanging around. Take my old Peugeot." Francis handed him the keys. "That cherry-red Mercedes of yours is too damn conspicuous."

"But shouldn't you go instead of me?"

"I'd be recognized for sure. Get moving. And Vincent . . . for God's sake keep this as quiet as you can. Don't tell anybody any more than they need to know—including the police."

THREE

I t was still dark in the Valley, but the red ribbon of
dawn widened a few inches and shifted into orange.
    Its tires crunching on the gravel, the Peugeot
rolled down the driveway to the narrow asphalt lane running between Château Letessier and the vineyard of
Stag's Leap Wine Cellars. As Vinnie stopped at the edge
of the lane, he saw the jogger again, running back toward
the hills to the east. As usual, she was running at the
crack of dawn; but this time, peering through the dark-
ness, he got the impression she might be pretty. He hoped
so. At least she had the trim figure of a runner. But this
was no time . . .

    He turned right onto the asphalt and right again onto
the Silverado Trail, heading north toward St. Helena,

passing the Pine Ridge Winery on his left and the steep hillside plantings of Shafer's Vineyard up in the eastern hills on his right. At Zinfandel Lane he turned left until he reached Highway 29—dignified as Main Street while passing through town, then becoming Highway 29 once more.

Turning right again, he drove up Main, looking for the St. Helena police station. *Can't miss it,* his uncle had said. *Right next to the city park.*

He missed it anyway. He drove past something that looked as if it could have been a park—a small plot of ground with trees and grass. A gazebo, or a bandstand, stood under the trees, and there was a good-sized rock by the sidewalk with a bronze plaque on it—but the place seemed too small to be a city park, and anyway there was no police station. Instead, he saw a one-story stucco building where they sold ice.

Vinnie drove on. He began to panic only when he reached York Creek and the Beringer Vineyards. Another half mile would bring him to the Christian Brothers winery, and that would wrap it up for St. Helena.

He turned around and headed back toward downtown, taking it slow, his eyes darting right and left this time. He passed the house near the corner of Madrona and Main where that terrific-looking chick who worked in the bank lived. Probably Italian, possibly Greek. Black hair, but very un-Italian blue eyes. Lombards were probably responsible for that. He recognized her station wagon in the driveway, full of shiny helium balloons, wished he was invited to whatever party it was (unless it was a kid party), and then felt ashamed of himself for thinking about chicks at a time like this. The words around her license-plate frame read MILLIONAIRE IN TRAINING—very blah; not like the funny one he saw yesterday that said, I'M NOT A BRAT—I'M NOT, I'M NOT, I'M NOT! But this was also a hell of a time to be thinking about license plates.

He drove past Vasconi Drugs and the Model Bakery

12

and the Masonics Building, the St. Helena Hotel, and a cookery-wine-and-gift store called Bah Humbug. It irritated him that the trash cans along Main Street were concealed in wine barrels. Too cutesy. He didn't want to notice trash cans; he wanted the goddamn police station. When he reached the bridge over White Sulphur Creek, he knew he had gone too far south, and then he really panicked. He pictured Uncle Francis standing next to that purple corpse in the fermentation room, waiting, waiting . . . His mouth went dry and his gut clenched. He turned the Peugeot around and headed north once more. The sky was now the dark gray of dirty dishwater.

Maybe that small square with the trees in it had been the city park after all. Maybe the police station shared that small building with the icehouse or whatever it was at the corner of Main and Pine Street.

Ice*house?* The painted sign on the side of the building said it was a *department*—that is, the sign read ICE DEPT.. . . . Good god!

Vinnie parked the Peugeot around the corner on Pine Street and was relieved to see a police car and a fire engine parked on the concrete driveway at the side.

The policeman in blue behind the desk was named Bailey.

"Sorry about that," said Bailey with a grin. "They haven't finished painting that wall yet. How can I help you, sir?"

"I need to report a dead body—a man."

Bailey gave him a quick glance. "Yes, sir. May I have your name, please?"

Vinnie identified himself and Bailey swung around to the log sheet in his typewriter.

"What kind of dead body?"

"What do you mean?"

"Look like he was murdered, drowned, OD'd, or what?"

"I guess murdered."

13

"What makes you think so?"

"Gee, I don't know." Vinnie felt silly, the way he had in his M.A. oral when he couldn't remember Molière's real name. "We just assumed."

"Where'd you find this body?"

"In the fermentation room. At the winery."

"Which winery?"

"Château Letessier."

"What time?"

"About an hour ago."

"Were you acquainted with the deceased?"

"No. We don't know who he is."

"Who's 'we'?"

"My uncle and I."

"Your uncle being Francis Letessier?"

"Right. So—you'll send a detective up?"

"Not from here, no."

"How come?"

"First of all, your winery isn't in St. Helena, it's county." (Like most locals, Bailey pronounced it "Sane Aleena.") "You'll have to drive down to the Hall of Justice in Napa and talk to a deputy sheriff."

"Not a detective?"

"A deputy sheriff in Napa *is* a detective. They call themselves 'investigators,' but a couple of them are homicide detectives—that is, if this homicide of yours is a homicide."

"Christ. Is there a phone here I can use? I better call my uncle."

"Right over there."

Uncle Francis engaged in a good deal of bilingual cursing before Vinnie hung up. "My uncle wonders if you'd do him a favor and not put this on the air—on the radio. He says reporters are always listening."

Officer Bailey grinned. "And how right he is. Okay, fine. All I'll do is enter it on my blotter here. Hall of Justice in Napa is at Eleven twenty-five Main—officially,

14

that is, but the address won't do you any good. Just go down Twenty-nine and turn left on Third Street till you see it."

"Left on Third."

"If you fall in the Napa River you'll know you've gone too far. But you can't miss it—and they don't sell ice there either."

Vinnie gave the humorist a bleak smile.

Hyperalert now, crouched over the steering wheel as he rolled southward into the city of Napa, Vinnie carefully registered First Street, took note of Second Street, nailed down the fact that Third did indeed come after Second, turned left, and was not fooled even when Third tried to pull a fast one on him by shooting off at a tricky oblique angle where Church Street intersected it.

The Hall of Justice looked like one of the newer buildings at UCLA, a modern mixture of cut stone, plate glass, white parabolic arches over the office windows on the upper floors, and a red brick sidewalk and patio in front; but Vinnie was too wrought up to appreciate architecture or the stone bench under a liquidambar tree or the clumps of heavenly bamboo in planter boxes.

Seeing light down a hallway, he followed it to a room, almost deserted at this hour, full of desks, papers, and filing cabinets. Two people sat at desks against the far wall, a burly man whose muscles bulged in his short-sleeved white shirt, and a petite and pretty young woman to the right, wearing a similar white shirt and a bolo tie with a Navajo silver-and-turquoise clasp. Before Vinnie could say a word, telephones rang on both desks.

"Investigations, Black," said the man.

Vinnie assumed that the woman was the department secretary, from the way she answered her own phone. "Sheriff's Investigations, Holly Shelton speaking, may I help you, please?"

While Detective Black took a report concerning stolen livestock, some citizen was informing Holly Shelton of a hidden marijuana patch. She took shorthand notes and thanked the citizen for helping to make at least a small inroad on California's number one cash crop.

The secretary hung up and looked at Vinnie. "May I help you?"

"Um, well, there's a dead body—uh, looks like a murder . . ." Vinnie shot glances at Detective Black, but Black was still talking and showed no sign of being about to finish. Vinnie's head swiveled back again when the woman spoke.

"I'm a homicide detective—among other things."

"You *are!* Not—? I mean—well . . ." Vinnie looked briefly into the blue eyes of Detective Shelton. The blue eyes stared unblinkingly back, waiting for Vinnie to get it out of his system—his shock at encountering a petite, 5'3 detective who had shoulder-length hair the color of dark honey and the complexion of a porcelain doll. Evidently she had been through this before. Stammering only a little, he gave her the details, which she typed into the log: "90-0401096—0651—POSSIBLE HOMICIDE—Vincent LETESSIER reports dead body, white adult male, at Château Letessier, 944–5027. Detective Shelton responding."

She got up, thrust a snubnose Smith & Wesson .38 Airweight revolver into a tiny holster at the small of her back, put on a jacket, and grabbed an equipment kit and a Polaroid camera.

"Okay, let's go view the remains."

FOUR

U ncle Francis was waiting in the open doorway of the fermentation room. He clenched his fists when he saw his nephew approaching with a cutie-pie.

"What the hell have you been doing, Vincent? Where are the police?"

"Uncle—this is Inspector Shelton from Homicide."

"Are you trying to be funny?"

"Flash your buzzer, Inspector," said Vincent, an Ed McBain fan.

She gave both of them a dirty look, but showed her badge.

"Well, excuse me—*Inspector* Shelton."

"Call me Miss Shelton or Shelton or even Holly, if it makes you more comfortable. Where's the corpse?"

"This way," said Francis, turning to enter the fermentation room.

"Stop right there!" said Holly. "Both of you wait here."

"Why?" said Francis. "Don't you want me to show you?"

"I know what a fermentation room looks like, Mr. Letessier, and I don't want the scene messed up any more than it is."

"No clues are lying around, if that's what you're worried about."

"Oh? What do you call that?" said Holly, pointing to the corpse.

"Oh, well *him,* sure, but there's nothing more."

"You're wrong. There always is." She broke out her camera and began photographing the general scene. "Nobody can come into a place—any place at all—without changing it in some way, even if all they leave is some hair or gum wrappers. It's called the Locard Exchange Principle, if you want to be technical."

Uncle and nephew looked on with interest as Inspector Shelton carefully moved toward the body, watching where she walked and taking several more snapshots. Finally, she stood looking down at the body, her hands on her hips, disgusted.

"Don't you two ever read detective stories? You should know better than move a body. All right, who pulled him out of that tank?"

"I started to," said Vinnie, "and then we did it together."

"And *why* did you pull him out of the tank?"

"Well—I guess we—just didn't want him in there."

"Jesus Christ."

"What does it matter anyhow?" said Francis. "In or out, he's dead."

His comment went into Holly's mental Dumb Questions folder, but she said nothing. Opening her equipment kit, she took out a rubber roller, an ink pad, and an assortment of small cards for taking fingerprints, but before she began she looked up at the two Letessiers. "You did say you don't know who he is?"

"Never saw him before," said Francis.

She knelt by the corpse, inked the rubber roller and applied it to the fingers of the corpse's right hand. Her honey-colored hair fell forward on both sides of her face like a theater curtain closing, as she concentrated on her work.

Francis muttered through his teeth, "Since when do Barbie dolls get on the police force? And isn't there supposed to be a minimum height?"

"Beats me, Uncle. But take my advice and don't ask her."

They watched from a distance as Holly took two prints of each finger and carefully labeled the cards.

"This is interesting," she said. "You two can come down here now. But don't get between me and the fermentation tank."

When they were standing beside her she said, "Look at this." She bent the corpse's arm back and forth.

My god, thought Vinnie, *she's got it waving bye-bye!*

"Still flexible," said Holly. "It takes two to six hours for rigor mortis to set in, so our friend here hasn't been dead for long. Three o'clock in the morning shouldn't be too bad a guess." She frowned. "Unless . . ."

"Unless what?" said Francis.

"Unless the rigor has actually come and gone, which would mean he's been dead two or three days—but that makes no sense at all."

"Ridiculous," agreed Francis. "I suppose it's up to the coroner."

"I'm a coroner."

"Oh, now, come *on!*" Barbie as coroner?

"All sheriff's investigators in Napa County are deputy coroners. And we've got a *chief* deputy coroner. I know—it shocks a lot of people to see me sign a death certificate, but it's the truth. Of course, if I run into a really tough case I turn it over to a pathologist the county has under contract. Dr. Hardesty. I don't have to cut 'em up myself.''

"How about your customer on the floor?'' said Vinnie.

"I don't know about him yet. But I'll tell you one thing: Somebody sure doesn't like *you*, Mr. Letessier. It was bad enough to kill somebody in here—if this is where he *was* killed—but shoving him into the tank was a really dirty trick.''

With a piece of chalk she traced the outline of the body on the concrete floor. Lifting the hem of the Mexican wedding shirt, she gave the corpse's belly and chest a cursory inspection. Then she turned the body over, took more photographs, and glanced at the dead man's back.

"Nothing obvious. We'll have to wait for the autopsy. Meanwhile, we'll have to go through the rest of the muck in this tank and drain the tank you transferred the wine to.''

Francis scowled. "Do you have to do that? You're talking about thirty-nine hundred gallons of cabernet.''

"Of course. We're sure to find more evidence.''

Francis cleared his throat. "Look, Inspector Shelton. As you pointed out, this body was put in the tank just hours ago.''

"No, I only said it could have been.''

"But it had to be. At some time during the night, for sure.''

"Why?''

"This is Saturday morning. Fermentation was still going on Thursday, so he couldn't have been swimming around in the tank then. Right?''

"I don't see why not.''

"You've never seen fermentation at its height? It's a volcano! Carbon dioxide roars up through the grape skins and you couldn't stick a corpse in there if you tried all day. It'd pop up like a Ping-Pong ball. And I was up there several times Thursday checking the sugar level, so I would have seen him. And I sure as hell would have seen anybody lugging a corpse up the ladder!"

"And Friday?"

"Yesterday we clarified the wine—ran it through a filter and transferred it to another tank. So this body had to be shoved in afterwards, meaning last night—which accounts for the door being unlocked."

"Wait a minute! Somebody could have stuck the corpse in there yesterday after the fermentation stopped."

"No. Impossible. Too many people around. We would have seen something. If the body got in there after we transferred the wine—sure, we'll give *this* tank a hell of a cleaning, but there's no need to drain the other one, is there now?"

Holly bit her lip and thought it over. "What you say is plausible, Mr. Letessier, and if we lived in a reasonable world maybe I'd go along with you. But in a case like this, people are going to fall over backwards. They're going to demand absolute proof, and I don't think you or I or anybody can offer them that."

"What people?"

"You know very well who. Mainly the state Food and Drug Administration. You know how picky they are about any kind of contamination in winery tanks. They're worse than the Feds—the Bureau of Alcohol, Tobacco, and Firearms—but you could very well have both of them on your back."

"What if nobody gets them involved?"

"Now, *look*, Mr. Letessier—"

"Who says they have to know?"

"Number one, I do, because I don't want to lose my job. And number two, the public. I have to turn in a report, and what if there's an off-chance that body fluids have gotten into your wine—what a charming thought *that* is! But even if they haven't—even if all the tests say you're clean—if people start raising a stink, the authorities will drain those tanks just to satisfy public opinion.''

''You mean to cover their asses.''

''That's politics.''

''Meaning you intend to ruin me.''

''Look—we'll do everything we can to keep publicity at a minimum—not just for you but for all of us in the Napa Valley.''

''Yeah. Sure.''

''First of all we need to find out who the dead man was. Should be easy enough: California has a computerized system now for identifying fingerprints. Cal-ID, it's called.''

''Wonderful. A treat worth waiting for.''

''And then we'll nail the son of a bitch that did this. Have any ideas yourself?''

''Sure. Start with the Napa Valley phone directory.''

''You're not being very helpful, Mr. Letessier.''

''No? All sorts of people would like to see me go belly up—enemies, a couple of competitors, companies that want to buy the place. One or two people on the Board of Supervisors and the Planning Commission— who shall be nameless—just don't like me personally. Maybe even those teetotalling religious nuts up in Angwin. Then there's those two birds I fired who drained a tank of cabernet franc into the river. Also nameless since I can't prove it.''

''We know who they are, and I'll be checking up on them.''

''Everybody knows who they are. Meanwhile they're hoping I say something so they can bring a slander suit against me. As for the others, want them in alphabetical order? We could start with *A*—my beloved ex-wife Adrienne, along with her current *chouchou*.''

''*Chouchou?*''

''Tootsie wootsie. Heartthrob. My former resident

22

manager, George Preston. She ran off with a quarter million, you might say, and he ran off with her. The two of them are still living in St. Helena."

"In short," said Holly, "we're looking for someone either angry enough or greedy enough or crazy enough to do this to you. But another thought occurs to me: It's at least possible that two men broke in here last night, maybe planning to drain tanks again or vandalize equipment or do whatever would hurt you, and they had a falling-out. One kills the other one and shoves him into the tank—neatly killing two birds with one stone."

"An efficiency expert."

"Anyway, I think we'll learn a lot from the autopsy. Where will I find a phone? I'll go call an ambulance."

FIVE

embers of the crew came straggling up the path toward the fermentation room, but stopped in wonderment when they saw a body covered with a white sheet being wheeled out on a gurney. This was a sensational way to begin a workday, and they were full of questions, but the medics merely said they were giving a stiff a free ride into town.

Gil Fernandez, the foreman, hurried inside and joined Francis, Vinnie, and Holly Shelton at tank F17. He was appalled to learn why grape skins and purple juice were staining the cement, why a body had been outlined in chalk, and—above all—where that body had come from.

"Sangre de Cristo!"

25

"Let's get with it now," said Inspector Shelton. "Vincent, you can finish raking the pomace out of there—and Gil, I want it put in tubs. *Nobody* is to touch the stuff but the police. I'm also going to seal tank F20. Most likely it'll have to be drained, so nobody touches that either. Do you understand me?"

"I think I can grasp the concept, Holly."

The handsome Latino looked at the petite homicide detective with an amused smile. She did not smile back. She glared. Vinnie watched them with interest. Some sort of electricity—negative, positive, or grounded—oscillated between them.

Even in work clothes, Gil Fernandez looked like a Spanish hidalgo. He wore a khaki shirt that he must have had tailored—it fit so snugly at his narrow waist—and dark blue chinos. His belt buckle sported a mosaic flower, with petals of rose quartz circling a lapis lazuli center. His brown work shoes were *polished*. He was equally elegant physically. He had gleaming black hair, a narrow tan face, black eyebrows, and black eyelashes that girls would kill for. His white teeth flashed all the whiter against his tan.

"You two know each other," said Vinnie.

"We've met," said Holly.

"In an official capacity," said Gil with a grin. "Once in a while I ask her for a date, but Holly was my arresting officer once, and that got me off on the wrong foot. I don't think she likes rowdy *cholos* anyway. Or *cholos* in general."

"Now, look!" she said. "You're full of it on both counts—you are *not* a *cholo*, and I am *not* prejudiced, so drop it, okay?"

"Especially a *cholo* named Hermenegildo. 'Hermenegildo' just doesn't have that romantic ring, does it? 'Gil' takes some of the curse off, of course. What do you want us to do today, Mr. Letessier?

"Start bottling the '88 cabernet. Who knows? Maybe we'll even sell it."

"Okay, you guys," Gil said to three of his men who had followed him in, "let's get with it. *Arre! Pónganse changos!*"

"Mr. Letessier," said Holly, "please phone Detective Tom Black at the Hall of Justice in Napa, will you? The number is 253–4451. Here." She scribbled it on a page of her notebook and tore it off. "Tell him to come down here, and bring a roll of yellow crime-scene tape. I forgot mine. I'll be staying right here."

Francis turned to go.

"Shall I finish raking the pomace now, Uncle Francis?" said Vinnie.

"Je m'en fous du pomace. Let it go till after breakfast—assuming I can eat any breakfast."

It was the frugal Continental breakfast familiar to tourists in France: A couple of croissants and brioches, pats of butter, *confiture de framboises,* cheese, café au lait. Mrs. Barton served it to them, but glumly. Brought up on a farm in Howard County, Missouri, she thought the "Continental breakfast" was a scandalous misnomer. ("That's no breakfast for working people!") She was also glum because she saw black clouds piling up on the horizon. Francis nibbled glumly, also because of the clouds. He watched with quiet disgust as his nephew cheerfully bit off a horn of his croissant and applied butter and raspberry preserves to the stump.

"Will there be anything else, Mr. Letessier?"

"No, thank you, Mrs. Barton."

He sipped his café au lait and eyed his nephew. "Vincent, do you happen to know what a spreadsheet is?"

"Unless it's what Mrs. Barton puts on my bed, no."

"How about a balance sheet?"

"Uh, shows how a business is doing, doesn't it? Debits and credits and all that?" Vinnie extracted a hand-

27

kerchief from his back pocket and wiped a smudge of butter off his black horn-rims.

Francis contemplated his nephew.

"You're very much the liberal arts type, aren't you, Vincent?"

Vinnie smiled.

"Which helps explain," Francis went on, "how both you and my brother ran through your inheritance so fast. It was the commodities market for Maurice, wasn't it?

"Was it ever! Dad bought and sold and bought and sold and bought and sold. Afterward, he told me he'd forgotten one thing—instead of paper profit at the end of the line, somebody owns a mountain of *real* soybeans or whatever."

"So he lost his shirt and died."

"Well, you could say he was never the same after that."

"And then it was your turn."

"I know, I know. It took a few years. My accountant kept telling me I was running out of money but I didn't take him seriously. Then they came and took away the furniture and piano and VCR and left me sitting on an orange crate up in Beverly Glen." Vinnie reminisced a moment or two as he buttered his croissant. "I didn't mind the piano so much—couldn't really play it anyway. Oh well, fun while it lasted."

"Fun."

"I just never could get interested in the world of finance," Vinnie went on. "Boring. Baffling. Once in a while I'd notice something really weird. Like down in L.A. I saw a building with a big sign on it that said 'Buffalo Reinsurance Company.' It got me to wondering why buffaloes had to be reinsured. And who let the original insurance lapse. Mind you, I know I had the whole thing wrong, but that's how my mind ran."

Francis glanced heavenward but forbore saying anything.

28

Vinnie gazed through the sliding glass doors at the valley floor and the distant hills. "The view out there is really rad, Uncle Francis."

"Rad?"

"You know, like, too much. Radical. Beautiful. Those neat vineyards with all those rows of green vines fanning out in a pattern. And then hills and trees and bushes all around. Combination of neoclassical and Romantic. Order surrounded by untamed nature. My favorite kind of landscape."

"Aaaagh!"

Vinnie jumped. "What's the matter?"

"Your goddamn cat just went by with a big rat in his mouth!"

"Ezra? Great! I told you he was grateful to be here. He wants to earn his keep too."

"Well, the son of a bitch doesn't do much for my appetite. What a hell of a day this started out to be."

The next day was far worse, and the cat had nothing to do with it.

SIX

But before the merde hit the *ailes de ventilateur* the next morning, as one might say in Pont-à-Mousson, rose petals hit the fan for Vinnie. He was standing on the flagstone patio outside the breakfast room with his hands in his pockets, breathing the cool September air, and watching the early morning sunlight slant through the vineyard and turn the grape leaves into blades of green fire.

Far lovelier, and more exciting, he saw, off to the west, the mysterious female jogger crossing the Silverado Trail at an easy lope and coming toward him. She was late this morning. In this light, and even a hundred yards away, he could tell she was pretty, perhaps even beautiful, although at this distance her features were blurred, like those of a woman in a French Impressionist painting.

Inspired, Vinnie hurried back into the breakfast room, plucked three golden delicious apples from a bowl on the refectory table, and hustled down to the edge of the asphalt lane. The young woman paced closer, her black shoulder-length hair bouncing as she ran. She glanced at Vinnie. He smiled and tossed the golden apples into her path.

She stopped in her tracks. Feet apart and hands on hips, she looked with curiosity at this young man with the black horn-rims and burnt-orange cashmere sweater.

Finally, she spoke.

"Well, Hippomenes!"

Aha! Vinnie's heart surged.

"Well, Atalanta!"

They smiled at each other. She brushed her hair back over her ears. Beneath her black bangs, beneath the gentle black eyebrows, and beneath the black eyelashes, her blue eyes—gentian blue eyes—scrutinized him. Young as she was, little crescent-shaped folds under her eyes suggested that either she hadn't been getting enough sleep or she had experienced more than a few of life's troubles.

He glanced at her hands. He was relieved to see an opal on her right ring finger and nothing on the left one. Her bare legs were pale. That was to be expected. Tan legs are rare north of San Francisco. She wore white shorts and a white sweatshirt with a red cow's face on the front, labeled VACHE QUI RIT above and LAUGHING COW below.

The young woman's lips parted in a more open smile, revealing perfect white teeth. A pink rose full of snow.

"You're something of a rare bird," she said. "Not many people around here ever heard of Atalanta."

"Not many of 'em are named Hippomenes either. For now, though, I go under the name of Vincent Letessier. Or Vinnie."

"I know you do." They shook hands. "I'm Peggy Singletary. And may I ask why you stopped me—Hippomenes?"

"I wanted to give you some advice—about jogging."

"Oh?"

"You're holding your arms too high and that makes you tense up. Keep doing that and you're sure to end up with hunched shoulders. You've got to relax, let your arms dangle more."

"How do you know all that? Are you a runner too?"

"No, tennis. But a physical therapist at UCLA—well, she's premed now—anyway, she told me about it. A woman named Mona Dunbar."

"So you stopped me because you're concerned about my health."

"Well, yes."

She gave him an impish smile. "Taurine meadow muffins, if you'll pardon my French."

He laughed. "Okay—so I wanted to meet you. And if the chemistry or physics or whatever was right, I hoped maybe we could get together. What do you think?"

"Sure. How about dinner at my place on—let's see—Friday evening, the twentieth?"

"The *twentieth?* Two weeks? You must have a lot of dates."

"I don't have any. I'm a custom-tile designer, and I'm doing a big mural for a winery and they're having a big international gourmet party on the nineteenth, and if I don't have the mural on the wall by the nineteenth I don't get paid that day, and if I don't get paid I can't buy groceries and it'll be Kraft dinner flambé for you instead of *mignonnette d'agneau.*"

"Okay, okay, I'll wait!"

"Make it seven-thirty. I live in a little house on Loma Vista. One-eighteen. You can see it from here if you look down in a straight line from the top of Stag's Leap." She pointed to a small white square among the distant oak trees.

"Can I bring anything?"

"Your appetite; and since you're trying to make a big impression, see if you can smuggle out a bottle or two of your uncle's '82 cabernet sauvignon. That was a *big* wine. Which I can't afford."

"I'll be there."

"Well . . . see you then."

Peggy jogged away eastward once more.

"Thanks!" Vinnie called after her.

She waved without looking back.

"Hey!" he called. "The French for those meadow muffins would be *merde de taureau!*"

He could tell she laughed.

In the afternoon, Detective Shelton drove up in a sheriff's department car with news about the corpse. She conferred with Francis and Vinnie in the breakfast room.

"Your corpse wasn't murdered at all. His name was Richard Mifflin and he died of heart failure several days ago over at Vacaville State Prison. He was an inmate."

"Vacaville! Where Charles *Manson* is? He died *there?*" said Francis. "But—wait a minute! If he died *there,* how in hell did he get *here?*"

"That's what we need to find out. Somebody brought him here and shoved him into that tank."

Uncle and nephew mulled the implications of this news.

"So this isn't even a homicide," said Vinnie.

"It's still a felony, though," said Holly.

"It's worse!" said his uncle. "It means somebody went to one hell of a lot of trouble to ruin me!"

'True," said Holly. "Someone in your circle of acquaintances, Mr. Letessier, is a certified, double-dyed, son of a bitch."

"But stealing a body! Who ever heard of stealing a body—at least these days?"

"It happens," said Holly. "My favorite is when Errol Flynn stole John Barrymore's body out of a mortuary and smuggled it into the Beverly Hills Hotel for a farewell drinking party. But don't worry, we'll find out who did this. We have a few clues."

"Such as what?"

"For starters, we know the cadaver was slated to go to a medical school in San Francisco, so somebody was probably bribed either there or at Vacaville. We'll be checking at both ends. Mifflin had no known relatives. We didn't find anything in the pomace Vincent raked out, but that peculiar Mexican shirt on the body—the pants are prison issue but that shirt certainly isn't, and it has a faint laundry mark we're trying to run down. A small fragment of what appears to be silver Mylar was stuck to the guy's belt. And there were carpet fibers in his shirt and pants that we'll try to track to the source."

"What about that Mylar?" said Vinnie. "What's it used for?"

"Solar-energy reflectors, thermal blankets, balloons, one-way glass, even saltwater fishing lures. Lots of things. But don't worry—chances are good we'll find out who did this."

"A fat lot of good that will do me," said Francis.

"Maybe if you're lucky it'll be somebody rich you can sue."

"Oh yes, and in eight years I collect the money. Meanwhile, I've gone down the drain."

Holly ran her fingers through her hair. "I'm sorry to bring such bad news, Mr. Letessier."

"At least it can't get any worse."

"I'm afraid it can. We definitely do have to drain your tank of cabernet." She bit her lower lip. "And I'm sorry to say the reporters have got wind of this. It'll hit the papers tomorrow."

"Oh, my god!"

SEVEN

T he Napa and Sonoma Valley newspapers treated the incident as an outrage and expressed their sympathy. The San Francisco papers treated it as a straight news story whose pathos spoke for itself. Reporters and editors in Los Angeles and points east, however, seized on the chance for some easy humor. Most of them hit on the same sort of gags. A story in the front section of the *Los Angeles Times,* for example, under the headline BODY IN WINE VAT HAS NAPA IN FERMENT, stated that "while many Napa Valley wineries are justly proud of their full-bodied wines, some oenophiles may feel that Château Letessier has gone too far. . . ." The *New York Daily News* observed that "there is lively disagreement among consumers, public health officials, and vintners

37

over the question of additives in wine, notably sulfites, but one Napa Valley winery has made a bizarre contribution to what we may call the body of oenological theory." A columnist in Dallas opined that it would only be poetic justice if the culprit who put the corpse in the cabernet "received a stiff sentence."

Uncle Francis could have taken this sophomoric buffoonery in stride, but not the bad publicity. Within days it became apparent that sales were plummeting for all Château Letessier wines, both red and white.

"That's crazy!" said Vinnie. "Do people really think a corpse could contaminate bottles of wine that've been sitting on market shelves?"

"I know what's running through their tiny little heads," said Francis. "They think, 'Ooo! If there's a dead body in *one* of their vats, who knows what's in the rest of them? Rats? Bats? *Cats?*' "

A week later a letter arrived from the San Francisco headquarters of the Canny Scot chain of elite grocery markets. Vinnie watched Uncle Francis slit the envelope open with a Swiss Army knife, read the message, and fling the letter onto the refectory table, where it came to rest on the butter.

"That pretty much does it," said Francis, rubbing his face.

"What did they say?" Vinnie asked.

"Read it."

The letter was from a Mr. Gary Underwood, vice president in charge of wine and spirits purchasing for Canny Scot. In the crucial paragraph Underwood expressed his great sympathy to Uncle Francis for the misfortunes that had befallen him through no fault of his own, but in view of Château Letessier's past inability to deliver the contractually agreed-upon quantity of 1987 cabernet (the tank the two malcontents drained into the Napa River), and in view of the inadequate supply of this year's estate-reserve cabernet that will be forthcoming, and in view of the recent disastrous publicity, and in view of the fact that Château Letessier's wine, while excellent in quality was always quite limited in quantity—all the more so now—it appeared advisable to terminate, with regret but on the most amicable of terms, the contractual relationship that Canny Scot and Letessier had enjoyed for the past six years. "Should circumstances improve in the future, we shall be only too glad to . . . etc., etc."

"Quick on the trigger, aren't they, the bastards," said Francis.

"How serious is this?"

"It's terrible. I've got one last ace in the hole, though, so I can hang on by my toenails for a while, but . . . Vincent . . . listen . . . if anything should happen to me . . ."

He broke off, pensive.

"Happen to you!"

"Life is uncertain—and whoever has it in for me might start playing for keeps. Who knows? But look, Vincent: Obviously, you'll inherit this winery some day. You and your cousin Delphine are the only relatives I have left—and I'm certainly not going to leave the place to Delphine and her *m'as-tu-vu* husband."

"Well, thanks, Uncle Francis, but I hope we're talking about forty years from now."

"J'en parlerai à mon cheval."

"No, I mean it—seriously! But you'd leave Delphine something, wouldn't you?"

"Of course. Oh, Delphine's all right—a little mouse but all right, but Bert Craven is a pain in the ass. Why she married him I don't know, but he thinks because she's related to me and he's a CPA, he's entitled to come over here and tell me how to run a winery. What he really wants is to be a partner. God, what a nightmare that would be!"

"You started to tell me something, though, about . . . well, in case . . ."

39

"Yes. *If* anything ever does happen to me, the first thing you should do is make Gil Fernandez your resident manager."

"How come you haven't done it yourself?"

"Because as I told you, I am *not* a nice guy. Fernandez is the best pruner in the Napa Valley, so I've always given him raises and kept him where he was."

"I don't get it."

"Get what?"

"The thing about pruning. Why is pruning such a big deal?"

Francis Letessier rubbed his bald spot and took a deep breath. "You do have a way to go, don't you, Vincent? Pruning is the most important job in the whole vineyard. *Everything* for the rest of the year—both quantity and quality of the grapes—depends on what's left on the vine after pruning."

"I thought they just cut the little shoots off and kept the strong stuff. You know—like roses."

"You did, did you? Well, along about January you'll see Fernandez and his crew at work. My method is trellising and cane-pruning, by the way, if that means anything to you, which I doubt. And next spring I'm putting in a few more acres of cabernet franc, so next summer—if we are both still here—you'll see Gil grafting cabernet franc buds onto the rootstock, and there never was a better man with a budding knife."

"Not sure I followed all that, Unk."

"I didn't think you would, but you'll learn. Oh— strange as it seems, I took on an oenology student from UC Davis last year who was damn near as good as Fernandez. A student! Bowled me over. The kid had a natural feel for it. He was good at everything else too."

"Did you hire him?"

"No, no, he was an intern. Most wineries add a student or two to their staffs. Temporary. This kid had a weird name—Dikran Arshagouni. He came from a rich

40

Armenian family, very aristocratic, so he refused to take any pay at all, which was all right with me."

"What was that ace in the hole you mentioned?"

Uncle Francis looked sharply at him. "Tell this to Adrienne's lawyers or the IRS, Vincent, and I'll have you declawed and castrated, you understand me?"

"I can keep a secret."

"See that you do. So—my last fifty thousand is stashed away in a special bank account in Vallejo. Maybe that'll tide me over for a month or two, maybe it won't. But I'll guarantee you one thing: The vultures and jackals have smelt blood by now and they'll start arriving on the doorstep at any moment. And I'll bet the first one will be Roy Ashton, a cold-hearted *salaud* from something called Triskelion Enterprises. The second one will probably be my dear nephew-by-marriage Bert Craven. Ordinarily he'd rush over to be first in line, but he'll play it subtle and come over second."

EIGHT

F rancis knew people, all right.
He and Vinnie sat together with Roy Ashton at
one end of a long mahogany table in the reception
room, a light and airy room on the western side of the
house. From the windows the eye traveled down the
slope, between the eucalyptus trees, past the fermentation room on the left and the storage and sales building
on the right, to the Silverado Trail below, paralleling the
slope.

The room was painted bone white. Two maps of
France hung on the wall behind Francis, who sat at the
head of the table. One was an antique map showing the
departments of France at the time of Napoleon, the other
a color-coded map of French wine-growing areas (red for

Bordeaux, yellow for Alsace, burgundy for Burgundy, rose for Anjou). A poster on another wall featured an enlarged photo of a brass plaque embedded in the pavement in front of Notre Dame cathedral, depicting a stylized compass rose and the legend "Point Zéro des Routes de France"—the starting point from which highway distances in France are measured. When Francis came to California and bought Château Letessier, he named his best cabernet sauvignon Point Zéro, his intention being that other wines would have to be measured against it, to their disadvantage. He now confronted the possibility that soon he might not be making any wine at all.

"Obviously, Mr. Letessier, you should sell now before your negative cash flow bleeds you white," said Roy Ashton.

"I'm not bankrupt yet, Mr. Ashton."

"You're close."

Vinnie found Ashton both interesting and disturbing to look at. The man had pale blue-gray eyes that seldom looked directly at the person he was talking to; they appeared to focus on something about a foot to the right of the other person's face—as if on a mote floating in the air, perhaps. His business suit was also blue-gray and his necktie dark blue, but his hair was a faded blond, combed straight back on his head as if hair were a bother—a nuisance to be kept out of the way. His voice was gray and matter-of-fact. It sounded to Vinnie like the distant voice on an answering machine saying, "Hello, you have *no* messages."

"Not so close that I'll give up without a fight," said Francis.

"Why fight at all? You can come out of this a rich man still, we get what we want, and everybody's happy. There's simply no problem as far as I can see." He glanced at Vinnie. "Your nephew appears to agree."

"No, he doesn't. He hardly knows what we're talking about."

"May I inquire why he's here, then?"

"He's been talking lately about the 'romance of farming' and how beautiful vineyards are."

"So?"

"I want him to see how romantic and beautiful this business is, and how romantic and beautiful *you* are."

Ashton's glance was stony. Vinnie wondered how the man could possibly avoid being angry, unless he held Francis in such contempt that he could feel no more than cold indifference.

"I understand your bitterness, but that's the way of the world, isn't it?" said Ashton.

"Vultures and carrion crow are also the way of the world."

"That too. But look here: You've got forty-seven acres, worth close to a million five; buildings, house, equipment, and wine on hand—*if* you can sell it—worth maybe another one million, maybe one-five. Your indebtedness—well, you know what that is better than I do. As for your cash position—you're floundering, aren't you? And then there's that five thou a month to your ex-wife, down the drain."

"You seem to know a lot about my business."

"It's my business to know. But my point is: Sooner or later, Mr. Letessier, you *are* going to sell. And I don't care whose offer it is, Triskelion will automatically top anybody's bid—any legitimate bid—by half a million. This means regardless of what happens, you will walk away with at least three quarters of a million after taxes. Is that so hard to take?"

"And what would I do with the money?"

"You tell me. Retire?"

"No, I'm a wine maker."

"Fine. Buy a small vineyard here that's easier to manage and enjoy your money. Possibly even in France. Someone in the office thought you might like to go back to your family roots in Touraine and produce *vouvray* again."

Uncle Francis smiled. "Ashton—a friend of mine had ten million dollars. His life's dream was to buy a yacht and live on it, but his wife absolutely refused. She hated the water and she hated him. So I said, 'Henry—*give* her five million and *leave*. Keep the other five and get your yacht.' 'No,' he said, 'I worked too damn hard for that money.' So he hung on for another five or six years but then he finally surrendered—gave her the five million and bought a beautiful yacht anchored in Sausalito. Lived on board for one month and died."

"The man was a fool, but what exactly is your point?"

Vinnie heard Uncle Francis mutter *"tête de lard,"* but his uncle replied with a grimace, "Ah well, let's say salt air is bad for you and leave it at that."

"Can I ask a question?" said Vinnie.

Both Ashton and Uncle Francis were startled.

"With all the money you guys have," Vinnie said to Ashton, "how come you want this winery so much? There must be a lot of other places you could buy up."

Ashton stacked his papers neatly and put them back in his attaché case. "The Napa Valley is a blue-chip, gilt-edge investment. There's a finite amount of land, the wineries are a tourist attraction, and the valley needs a first-class resort hotel for tourists to come to. Does that answer your question?"

"No. I just read in the *Wine Spectator* that the inns and B and B's around here average less than half full—like forty-eight percent. I don't know anything about finance, but that sounds like a rotten investment to me."

"Wait a minute. The Auberge du Soleil is good, but small. Meadowood is good but limited. The Wine Country Inn is quaint and all that, but *thousands* of tourists would like to stay here. So we're talking about a big first-class place with a dining room that will feature wine from its own vineyard—Château Letessier."

Uncle Francis rose out of his chair.

"Sorry you have to leave so soon."

Ashton smiled and gathered up his papers.

"I'll be back. And our offer will always stand: Triskelion will beat any legitimate offer by half a million."

"I will never sell. Never!"

"You will. And when the day comes you'll be glad to see me."

"*Va te faire foutre.*"

"I don't know French, Mr. Letessier."

"It means don't count on it."

Vinnie smiled. He doubted that Ashton's priapic equipment was long enough to follow through on Francis's suggestion.

As the sound of Ashton's stretch limo faded away, another car came crunching up the drive.

"Probably Bert Craven and your cousin Delphine," said Francis. "If so, the bastard is even more tactless than I thought."

But it wasn't Bert Craven. It was worse. It was Adrienne and her *chouchou* George Preston who emerged from a light blue '84 Cadillac Eldorado with white side-wall tires.

"Is that Adrienne's car?" Vinnie asked.

"No, Preston's, and nice key to his character it is. The Cadillac gives him prestige, but its age lets him pretend to be modest. Shifty bastard."

NINE

Vinnie had seen Adrienne's *chouchou* some three years back when Preston was still resident manager of Château Letessier, but had paid little attention to him then, and paid him less now—for sashaying toward him and his uncle, pelvis cocking to right and left like a church bell, was the sexiest looking woman Vinnie had ever seen.

Color was his first impression of Adrienne: red, white, tan, black—a cherry-red silk blouse and white shorts; tan legs, white socks, white tennis shoes; a billow of curly black hair. Tan arms, tan face. Up close, Vinnie saw how beautiful she was: Brown eyes in a heart-shaped face, black eyebrows, glossy cherry-red lipstick. A highlight on her lower lip glistened like a star.

But what made Vinnie's libido zero in on the Freudian basics was the low-cut red blouse, whose shirttails she had tied into a loose square knot between her breasts. Down below the knot, the asterisk of her navel drew his eyes to the smooth brown skin of her tight and muscled abdomen. Above the knot bulged her two brown mounds.

And her voice? Liquid. Melodious—but only in timbre, not text.

"Francis," she said, hipshot with her hands on her waist, "that last check of yours has bounced twice— twice! If you're trying to tell me something, I don't appreciate the message."

"I'll transfer some funds. Put it through again."

"No. What do you think it makes me look like at the bank—a check with all that rubber stamping all over it? And it doesn't exactly improve your reputation either, I might add."

"All right, I'll write you another one and put it in the mail."

"Today."

"Of course today. Why so worried? You can't be broke already."

"I won't dignify that. Is this your nephew?"

"Adrienne, Vincent. Vincent, Adrienne."

"I thought so. He looks a lot like you, but maybe it's just the black horn-rims. Neither one of you looks very French, I must say."

"We'll wear berets next time."

"Pleased to meet you, Vincent."

"*Je suis enchanté faire votre connaissance, madame.*"

"Jesus." She turned to go.

George Preston, keeping his distance, still leaned against the car on the driver's side. He wore gray slacks and a gray polo shirt that showed off his biceps. He was square-jawed, good-looking in a rugged way, with straw-colored hair bleached by the sun. From his six feet of height, he had a way of tilting his head back and narrowing his eyes, as if appraising the world, expecting to find it riddled with flaws, and seeing his opinion confirmed.

"Hello, George," said Francis.

Preston lifted a languid hand in salute.

"You've got a hell of a nerve showing up here," said Francis.

"You forget Adrienne doesn't drive."

"In the automotive sense, no."

"Very funny." Preston pushed off from the car and shoved his hands into his back pockets. "I want a word with you myself."

"Oh? What's on your mind?"

"Your mouth. Been doing a lot of talking, haven't you?"

"Ever since I learned English. But what's your beef?"

"I don't appreciate the way you've been bad-mouthing me."

"What are you talking about?"

"You know damn well what I'm talking about. You're trying to get me blackballed in this valley."

"What's the matter, can't find work?"

"No, I cannot, thanks to you. I'm damn good at my job, but every owner I talk to gives me a funny look and says there aren't any openings. It's been months, now. Fishy isn't the word for it."

"Maybe there aren't any openings. Ever think of that?"

"Come on, Francis! I can't even get a job pasting labels. Pretty obvious, isn't it? From what I hear, you've spread the word around the Vintners Association, you cheap son of a bitch!"

"George—number one, I'm not that powerful, and number two, I wouldn't do that to anybody—not even you."

"Bullshit. You can't hold on to a woman so you take

51

it out on me. But I'll give you a piece of advice: Knock it off—*now*—or you're going to be one unhappy son of a bitch! Come on, Adrienne." He opened the passenger-side door of the aging Cadillac for her, then got in and jammed the key into the ignition.

Francis came to the open window and put both hands on the door. "There's an old saying, George: Character is destiny. Think about it."

"Shit."

Preston gunned the motor and off they went.

Vinnie and Francis looked after the car, neither of them saying anything until it moved out of sight down on the Silverado Trail.

"Not happy, is he?" said Vinnie.

"Oh, the hell with him. He's always been a sorehead."

"Uncle Francis, can I ask a personal question? Of course, one look at Adrienne and I suppose the answer's obvious, but let's face it, man, she just doesn't seem like your type. So how come . . . well . . ."

"Why did I marry her? I was dazzled. No, not dazzled—obsessed!"

"I can see why."

"But she played it smart. She held me off—kept me at arm's length—because of her so-called 'moral upbringing in Vallejo.' Ha! I knew she'd make a rotten wife, but I was out of my mind—*plus fou que les fous*. The dumb truth is: *I absolutely had to go to bed with that woman!* Never mind the price tag, which turned out to be twenty-five thousand dollars per piece of ass, according to my calculations. And now we'll drop the subject, if you don't mind."

Vinnie dropped it.

Several hours then elapsed before Bert Craven and Delphine "thought we might drop in since we were passing by." Francis was not much pleased to see either one of them. He didn't like Bert. And Delphine—well, Delphine not only was the daughter of one of Francis's least favorite half-brothers back in Touraine, but also, though pretty, was dull—not stupid but closed in, with little to say. That was all right. At least she was decorative. Bert wasn't, and Francis would have liked him more if he *had* been dull. There was something about his eyes . . .

Because they were guests and relatives, manners trapped Francis into doing the right thing yet again and inviting them in. The four of them sat around a table in the breakfast room, where Mrs. Barton laid out grapes, St. André and fol amour cheeses, Canadian wheat crackers, and two bottles of Francis's cabernet sauvignon.

"*Salut,*" said Vinnie, lifting his glass to Delphine.

"*Salut.*"

"Been a while, Delphine. Two years? A little more—two years this June. How's it going? Do you miss Amboise?"

"*Sais pas.* Not much." She tapped the ash from the cigarette she held in the fingers of her right hand; in her left she clutched a pack of Virginia Slims and a lighter. She sat with her elbows pressed to her sides. "Perhaps if I had lived in the castle at Amboise I would miss it more." Her lips curved up at the corners in a bittersweet smile. Her chestnut-brown eyes glistened in her olive-tan face. Her black hair, combed tightly upward, broke out into a surf of curls on her forehead.

Vinnie had always been interested in Delphine's dark coloration. Obviously, Moors or Phoenicians or some marauder from far to the east had swept through France and humped, pumped, and dumped a few of the women on the mother's side of Delphine's family. Vinnie and Uncle Francis, like a few million other French, owed their appearance more to the Visigoths, who roared in and stayed because they liked France, its women, and its wine.

"How about the English lessons? Ready to give us a lecture on *Finnegans Wake?*"

She smiled a faint smile. "English is very difficult. I understand better, and read, but still I speak only a small—a little."

Bert brushed cracker crumbs off his sweater. "But don't humor her and start spouting French or she'll never learn."

"You could learn French from her," said Francis.

"No, thanks, I've got enough problems. So do you."

"So you're here with all the solutions."

"I have some ideas. Plus some friendly advice."

"Such as sell to Triskelion?"

"You could do worse. Maybe you could do better. Look—I'm a CPA, but it doesn't take a CPA to see you're in a bind."

At this point Bert shifted into his customary pattern of speech, ending phrases and sentences on a rising tone, usually raising both hands and sometimes shrugging his shoulders as if wishing people weren't so obtuse, but doubting they'd ever improve. He also shot one glance at Vinnie and dismissed him from the conversation as a nonentity.

"You're in debt to the *bank*, you pay heavy *alimony*, you've now lost three tanks of *wine*, you don't have a resident *manager*, you've got a dead *body*, and I'd guess your sales are dropping, right?"

"The body's gone, but yes—the memory lingers on."

"So what's your plan?"

"Muddle through and hope for the best."

"I thought so, and that's why you need somebody like me. Look, Francis, if you were as good a business-man as you are a wine maker, no problem. But you've got to combine the two, and even the way you go about wine making gets in the way of business."

"Oh? What do you think I do wrong?"

"It's not that it's wrong, you just don't look at the market *realistically*. You barrel-age your cabernet up to two years and bottle-age it two more—which is great, you turn out terrific wine—but meanwhile it's taking up room and the meter is ticking away on your storage costs. Most wineries age their stuff in barrels fifteen months to two years, and maybe add merlot to soften it and make it drinkable a lot sooner. They keep it moving—free up their storage capacity. Mind you, if you were as big as Ernest and Julio Gallo, no sweat—you'd have plenty of room for indulging your high standards."

"If I didn't make wine the very best I know how, I'd quit the business and raise table grapes. Thanks for the lesson anyway."

"Just trying to help. All I'm saying is you're about to go under and there's no need for it. There are several ways out."

"Such as—to repeat—selling out to Triskelion?"

"You could, but why not beat them at their own game?"

"What game?"

"The hotel. Look, you've got over forty acres here. Let's say you set aside twenty acres for a hotel. Depending on the size, it could be built for maybe ten *million,* you'd have a steady *income,* and you'd still have a twenty-acre *vineyard*—which you could easily manage without either me *or* a resident manager, know what I'm saying?"

"Bert, I've been here a long time. I came to this valley when Robert Mondavi was still Bob Mahn-dayvy —and I'm not about to cut myself in half."

"You wouldn't be."

"And if I'm about to go under, where do I get ten million dollars?"

"I have banking connections. What if I negotiated the financing and construction?"

"Merely out of the goodness of your heart?"

"I'd get a finder's fee. Five percent."

"Fifty thousand or more."

"You're quicker than I thought. So we'd both make

money. What's wrong with that? Tell you what: I'll even kick back part of the finder's fee. What do you say?"

"A lot. Number one, I know nothing about the hotel business."

"The backers will hire people and it'll run itself."

"Number two, you'd have a hell of a time getting this through the Board of Supervisors and the Planning Commission."

"I have connections there too. Don't tell anybody I said so, but your fellow Frenchman on the county board, Andy Lacroix—you might say he's a friend of mine, and half the time he's the swing vote on projects like this, know what I mean?"

"I wouldn't brag to anybody about having that *salaud* as a friend."

"*Salaud* or not—whatever that means—he's been a power on the board, keeping a balance between wine-growing and tourism."

"Which brings me to number three, these goddamn tourists. Know what we call them around here? 'Crows.' They're ruining the place, and my fellow Frenchman André Lacroix should rot in hell for his part in it. You know how many tourists come here every year? Two million! It's getting to be like Yosemite!"

"They also bring in a hundred and fifty million dollars."

"Yes, and they also bring their cars—and their smog, as if we don't get enough blowing up from San Francisco. Look at them this month! All those lines of cars on Highway Twenty-nine and the Silverado Trail! Traffic jams! Truckers had a hell of a time trying to get their grapes to the wineries for the crush. And you talk about building another hotel! So number four is no, over my dead body!"

"All right, all right, I get your point, but at least keep it in mind if push gets to shove. But there are other things you can do. Look—"

Bert extracted a yellow legal table and a yellow number 2 Ticonderoga pencil from a leather folder. "Let's start with the two main factors. You could call them the good news and the bad news. The good news is, your flexibility is a little better than okay. You could convert assets into cash without too much delay. For starters, you could sell what wine you have in your tanks to other wineries, who'd be glad to take it off your hands—at a loss, sure."

"Go on."

"Incidentally, it wasn't very smart of you to let your insurance lapse, either."

"Go on."

"Selling land would take a little longer, but plenty of buyers would give you a hefty cash down payment on the spot."

"I can hardly wait for the bad news."

"The bad news is, the longer you delay, the worse will be the ratio of your net income to sales. And *if* you delay you'll butt head on into two more deadly ratios: Your fixed assets to your current liabilities, and your current liabilities against your noncurrent liabilities—any balloon payments down the road, for example."

Vinnie twiddled his wineglass and tried to extract what entertainment he could get from smiling at Delphine, who gave him a wan smile in return and puffed on her Virginia Slim.

"Now, what you've been doing several times—or so I've heard—is financing your fixed assets with current debt—which *can* be *okaaay*—" (shrug of the shoulders, both hands lifted)—"but the problem there is that the debt comes due before you can realize the proceeds from the fixed assets."

"I don't intend to liquidate any fixed assets."

"You may have to. Look." Bert began scribbling numbers rapidly on the yellow pad. "Let's just say for the sake of argument that you sell forty thousand units of wine at ten dollars per unit—that's four hundred thousand—less cost of sales, including direct material, direct labor, variable overhead at, say, forty percent . . . gross margin . . . selling and administrative expenses . . . loan . . . refinance . . . points . . . subordinated debentures . . . a = CM/S . . ."

As Bert droned on, Vinnie's eyelids grew heavy, just as they did when, as an undergraduate at UCLA, he had the bad judgment to sign up for the one-semester course in financial mathematics, renowned on campus as Mickey Mouse. The results would have been disastrous had he not dropped out before midterm without penalty. But the experience prompted him to memorize a passage from S. J. Perelman (his favorite reading when he should have been reading Michelet's *Histoire de la Révolution Française*): "There is nothing like a good, painstaking survey full of decimal points and guarded generalizations to put a glaze like a Sung vase on your eyeball."

Vinnie's eyes glazed over.

"So I see only two alternatives," said Bert, by way of what Vinnie hoped was conclusion. "You can either sell the acreage—or I volunteer to come in as your business manager so I can figure a way out of this jam."

Bert laid down his pencil and gazed intently at Francis with round eyes and mouth dropped slightly open. He looked like a psychologist peering into a laboratory maze to see if the rat would make the correct turn to the left and encounter a female in estrus, or turn right into a blind alley and receive an electric shock.

"If you two will excuse me," said Vinnie, rising, "I'm going out for a little fresh air."

"Me too," said Delphine.

They went out onto the flagstone patio, Vinnie stretching his lanky frame as Delphine lit another cigarette.

"Do you get exposed to a lot of that?" said Vinnie.

"I have to listen to it all the time. I try to understand but it makes me sleepy."

"You and me both. Looking back, I can see maybe I shouldn't have majored in French."

"Why did you?"

"Oh, I just wanted to have fun in college. Money was no problem—ha!—then, that is. So I majored in French because I already knew it. Joined a fraternity. Partied with sorority girls. Got on the tennis team. Sounds pretty shallow to you, I suppose."

"Shallow? What is that *en français?*"

"*Superficiel. Sans profondeur.*"

"Perhaps. But I look at myself. I wanted to get away from Amboise, so I came to UC Berkeley to study interior design. I met Bert there and he proposed, and I liked him and I wanted to stay in America. So I too am *superficielle.*"

"Is your marriage okay?"

"Good enough. I stay amused. I do some interior decorating."

"How about Bert?"

"He's all right. He works very hard because he wants to be rich. He wants—everything. So, I believe he plays around from time to time, but he always comes back. I am his *point d'appui.*" Another wan smile appeared on her face. She tossed her cigarette into the ivy.

Francis and Bert emerged from the French doors onto the patio. Bert and Delphine said their good-byes and drove away.

"Vinnie," said Francis as they disappeared, "two pieces of advice: If you want to keep a friend, don't go into business with him. And *never* go into business with a relative."

Tourists appeared, wanting either to buy wine or rubberneck. Francis strode down to meet them, leaving Vinnie wondering who Bert played around with. One of the answers would surprise him later on.

TEN

The September evening had turned cool when Vinnie walked out of the house for his Friday date with Peggy Singletary. He wore the same outfit that had been a winner among the sorority women at UCLA: burnt-orange cashmere sweater, dark tweed slacks, brown Bally moccasins.

He was about to turn into the lane leading toward the hills when a car pulled over and the driver leaned out. It was Inspector Shelton.

"I'm on my way to another call, but I have a small piece of news on your case—mostly negative, sorry to say. We tracked down the laundry mark on Mifflin's—the body's—Mexican shirt."

"Find out who owned it?"

61

"Up to a point. A man in Napa named Gustafson put it in the Salvation Army collection box, but nobody in their thrift shop has any idea who bought it—so it's a blind lead."

"Oh well, at least you know it was somebody local."

"Right. We'll keep on it. Anyway, pass it on to your uncle and maybe to Gil—or should I say Hermenegildo"—which she strung out into "Air-menna-heel-do" with a touch of sarcasm.

She drove on and Vinnie made his way up the slope to Peggy's house. It stood on a side road that was little more than a trail, a tiny white clapboard house with a green roof, almost lost among a grove of valley oaks. The feathery leaves of a silk floss tree shaded the wooden porch. Vinnie walked up and rang the ship's bell that hung by the door.

Peggy came to the door wearing an apron, her black hair brushed and gleaming, a bright smile on her face.

"You're right on the dot."

"It's one of my faults," said Vinnie.

"I'd call it a virtue. Timing is everything when you're cooking. Come in, come in! Here, let me take those. Oh, you did it—the '82 cabernet! Does your uncle know you took these, or should you tell me?"

Vinnie watched her as she took the bottles to the kitchen, moving with the grace of a dancer. Her clothes, he thought, looked both casual and expensive for a working girl ("woman," he amended; got to be politically correct). Her blouse was white silk with long sleeves and a narrow collar, above an olive-brown twill skirt—wool, it seemed. A short strand of pearls drew the eye to her long and lovely neck.

"Nice ensemble," he said.

"Thank you. I order most of my clothes from Orvis in Virginia. They're just right for me and it's the one real luxury I allow myself. Can I fix you a drink? I don't have

62

hard liquor but I make a terrific boccie ball. Light, and it won't numb your taste buds."

"That's a new one on me. What is it?"

"A jigger of amaretto, lots of orange juice, and a little soda."

"Sounds great."

It was, he found. While she busied herself in the kitchen, he sipped the drink and examined her small living room. The couch he sat on, he suspected from the goosey springs, was an old one, concealed under a floral slipcover.

The pictures on the wall were all prints: Monet, Pissarro, Cassatt, Tamayo, Caillebotte, Matisse's *La Blouse Roumaine;* the white blouse and blue skirt on the model in the Matisse reminded him of Peggy herself. Next to the doorway into the kitchen hung a Georgia O'Keeffe poster from the Santa Fe Music Festival, the music being represented by a joyous, curling wave in red, rose, pale blue, white, and yellow.

"Well, Hippomenes!" she said, sitting in an armchair opposite him and sipping her boccie ball. Her blue eyes peered at him below her black bangs. "Let's skip the weather, religion, crops, and politics and get down to you. I'm curious to know about you. Oh—but first let me say I feel terrible over the trouble at your winery. It's the worst thing that's happened around here in a long time."

"Which trouble? The body?"

"Of course! Have they found out anything?"

"All they know is, somebody stole a convict's body on its way from Vacaville to San Francisco and stuck it in the tank. Detective Shelton just told me it was wearing a shirt somebody unknown gave to the local Salvation Army. And that's about it."

"Holly Shelton? I've seen her around. She's sharp, isn't she?"

"I'll say. And tough. I'd hate to have her after me for something. . . . I'd much rather have *you* after me."

"Would you now?" Dimples appeared beside her mouth, which, he noted, was shaped sort of like a slice of red apple—no Cupid's bow at all—and the corners of her mouth were always turned up slightly, as if she were generally pleased with the world. It dawned on him that her prettiness was really far more beautiful than Adrienne's lush beauty. A paradox. Adrienne was a sexpot. Peggy had character. Substance.

"Tell me something about yourself," she said. "What brought you to the Napa Valley?"

"Bankruptcy."

She laughed in surprise. "Really?"

"Yeah. I was at UCLA and I ran out of money. I had no place to go but up here."

"Couldn't you have gone to work?"

"Ha! I never worked a day in my life until I joined my uncle."

"You're kidding."

"Nope—I've always been a card-carrying wastrel."

She laughed again. "You're certainly open about it."

"Oh yeah. *Je ne foqueronnes pas.*"

"I had two years of French but I don't know that one."

"It's a verb I made up for American consumption: I don't *foqueronne,* you don't *foqueronne,* he, she, or it doesn't *foqueronne.*"

"Uh huh. Well, tell me how you came to be a wastrel."

"Want my life in a nutshell? Okay. My grandfather was a rich vintner in Vendôme—that's in Touraine. He made *vouvray.* Left his money to my father and my uncle; they came to America; my uncle came here, my father to L.A. My uncle founded Château Letessier. My father put a lot of money in a trust for me, and played the commodities market. He lost a lot of money and I spent a lot of money. Toward the end, he bought fifteen contracts of pork bellies on what he thought was a hot tip—that's six hundred thousand pounds—three hundred tons of pork!—just as an investment. He sort of forgot that when the game of musical chairs is over, somebody is actually stuck with all that stuff—silver or cocoa or hogs or whatever it is."

" 'Hogs are steady,' " said Peggy. "I always got a laugh out of business reporters on the radio saying 'hogs are steady.' We don't want the poor dears staggering around and falling, do we?"

"Right. Nobody likes a wobbly hog."

"But go on about your father."

"What he did was wait just one day beyond the last selling day, and I'll never forget the look on his face when somebody phoned him from the freight yards at Union Station and said, 'Mr. Letessier, your pork bellies are here.' "

"What on earth did he do with them?"

"He didn't bring home the bacon, that's for sure. He sold them at a terrific loss to a packing company, and died not long after that. . . . my mother died several years ago, by the way."

"That's tragic! So you were left an orphan, but with money?"

"Sure. Meanwhile, I was majoring in French because I already spoke it. Played tennis. Partied. I had so much fun I didn't want to leave, so I went on to graduate school. Got as far as the M.A. exams."

"And?"

"The French department got tough. They asked me to give an explication de texte of Marcel Proust. I can't even *read* Proust. Talk about instant Halcion! How do you like thirty pages explaining how he turned over in bed? They asked me who I thought were the best French writers and I said Gabriel Chevallier and Marcel Aymé. That pissed them off, if you'll pardon my English. Hell, I knew they wanted me to say Balzac or Hugo or Flaubert, but instead I told them how I really felt."

65

"What did they do to you?"

"Gave me a terminal M.A., discouraged me from further graduate work, and more or less suggested I go work in a gas station."

"So your father lost his money. How did you lose yours?"

"Spent it."

"All of it?"

"Yep. I always thought when you needed money you just wrote a check. My accountant used to warn me I was running low, but I didn't take him seriously. And then one day he told me I was flat broke. That came as a shock. So I loaded my suitcase and my cat Ezra into my Mercedes and came here. End of story."

"Fascinating. I'm just the opposite. I've had to struggle for every penny."

"So what do you think about us wastrels? Disgusted? Eaten with envy?"

"Oh, no. Why hold it against you? You were born with a silver spoon in your mouth and life yanked it away. Either way, life isn't just, is it? Grumbling about it is a waste of time and energy, so I merely put on blinders and get on with what I want to do."

"You're a philosopher."

"*Je ne foqueronnes pas.*" Peggy smiled and sipped her boccie ball. "You wouldn't know it from that couch you're sitting on, Vinnie, but I've got it made. I design custom tiles and I love it and I own my own house, such as it is, and I too have a master's degree—in fine arts, from UC Santa Barbara."

"Aha! Two masters getting together!"

"And I got this big mural job from Clos d'Ausone— so big I had to buy a second six-hundred-dollar kiln on a credit card—but now I've been paid, which is why tonight we're having *mignonnette d'agneau au persil et aux champignons* instead of Kraft dinner flambé. *Très français, n'est-ce pas?*"

"Hey! Not a bad French accent! Choke a little more on those *r*'s and they'll think you're Parisian."

"*Mer-ci,*" she said, squeezing her epiglottis.

"Did you know there's a Château Ausone in France? At St. Emilion?"

"Oh, yes. Both of them are named after an old poet named Ausonius. That's why the owners had me put a Latin poem of his in the mural."

"I wish I could chip in on the dinner," said Vinnie, "but I'm broke."

"You've done more than chip in. That '82 Point Zéro cabernet sells for eighty-five dollars a bottle. So—shall we?"

They rose and went into dinner, sitting opposite one another in the breakfast nook. Along with the lamb, Peggy served asparagus with sesame seeds and glazed carrots.

"I can't believe this!" said Vinnie. "I haven't had a dinner like this since I was in France! How do you do it?"

"Just follow the recipe. The lamb is from Paul Bocuse's cookbook, the asparagus from Pierre Franey, the carrots from Fredy Girardet, and the wine from Château Letessier. All very French."

"Peggy—enough of this bourgeois badinage. Will you marry me? I may be broke and a wastrel but I've got prospects."

She laughed. "I thought you'd never ask. But hadn't you better wait till you can afford a ring?"

"I'll start saving up tomorrow. It won't take long, with me knocking down a cool fifty bucks a week."

After a simple but almost incredible orange soufflé, again out of the Bocuse cookbook, the conversation turned to The Body in the Tank.

"You've been around here a long time," said Vinnie. "Do you have any gut feeling about who might have done this?"

"About the kind of person, yes. Obviously, somebody wants to ruin your uncle, either for revenge or out of greed. The revenge part is easy, unless your uncle has made enemies we don't know about."

"You mean the two guys that drained his tank of cabernet?"

"Maybe. Everybody in the valley knows who they were—'Doc' Black and Joe Yates—but nobody can prove anything. But *since* everybody knows, I doubt they'd even be seen within a mile of the winery. No, I think they're out."

"Who else?"

She compressed her lips and her blue eyes looked up, slant-wise, toward a corner of the ceiling. Her black eyebrows also moved up and almost joined beneath her bangs. Vinnie felt his heart surge at the sight; it was one of those chance moments that have an impact on people for no reason they can explain but sometimes alter the course of their lives.

"Have you any idea how beautiful you are?" he said, leaning forward.

"How nice of you to say so! . . . but hadn't we better stick to the subject? If I were Holly Shelton I know I'd want to talk to Adrienne Letessier and George Preston. Both of them left the winery snarling and lashing their tails. However, neither one of them strikes me as the criminal type, but you never know."

"Right, you never know. Every once in a while down in L.A., some Eagle Scout walks up a slope with his rifle and takes potshots at drivers on the freeway. The neighbors are always shocked. 'He's such a *nice* boy!' they always say. 'Goes to Sunday school, carries a clean handkerchief, and keeps his hands to himself.' "

"We had one of those here not long ago. A student at that religious college over the hill in Angwin went a little crazy and shot at winery trucks and vineyard workers. He said he was declaring war on wine."

"Wonder what he would have said about Jesus turning water into wine at the wedding feast."

"They claim it was only grape juice."

"A likely parable. What were you going to say about greed?"

"Now, with *that* you get dozens of suspects," said Peggy.

"Care to mention any names?"

"Not really. But let me ask you something personal. How close are you to Bert Craven? Kissing cousins?"

"God, no. I don't even like him."

"Good. Neither do I. He strikes me as a man who wants to own the whole Napa Valley—including me, as I know from experience."

Vinnie felt sudden jealousy. "What did he do?"

"Oh, I passed him once when I was jogging, and he sort of leered and said, 'Hey, shall I run too?' and I said fine, as long as it's in the opposite direction. He just laughed. But later at a winery party he made a heavy pass at me, groping hands and all."

"Delphine hinted at something like that."

"I brushed him off, so he went after Nilla Toscana—with a little more success. She works in the bank in St. Helena. Anyway, two large groups of people would like to get their hands on your uncle's winery. Other vintners, for one. And these days it seems to be the chic thing to have your own wine label, so movie stars and stockbrokers and God knows who-all try to buy wineries even if it's just for a tax write-off. And then there are the big corporations—whiskey distillers, the Japanese, companies that make bleach and detergents, and people who want to build hotels or whatnot."

"Like Triskelion."

"I don't know that one, but there are others. What I'm getting at is—and I may be doing the guy an injustice—rumor has it that Bert Craven . . . oh, I should really keep my mouth shut. It's just gossip."

"I get your point anyway," said Vinnie.

"I'll mention one name, though, of somebody I *really* don't like: Andy Lacroix, who's on the Board of Supervisors."

"Uncle Francis doesn't like him either."

"I'm not surprised. Lacroix is popular with a lot of people, and disliked by a lot of others. He claims he tries to strike a balance between the old rural Napa and the new Napa by supporting the agricultural preserve, but then he'll turn around and vote for some big commercial development."

"How did a Frenchman ever get on the Board?"

"That's easy. He's from Bordeaux, so people thought he knew all about wine; he was a fighter in the French Resistance; and now he's become more American than Ronald Reagan—as you'll find out if you ever meet him."

"Don't think I want to."

"I think he has his eyes on something far bigger than the County Board, whether it's a winery or a share in a hotel or just a huge under-the-table bribe, I don't know. And now I think I will keep my mouth shut."

"Thanks for the education, anyway."

"You're welcome. And now let's talk about something pleasant, for heaven's sake."

"Yeah, like you, for instance. You said something when we met about not having many dates. I don't understand how that's possible. You're beautiful, and there must be other men around here besides Bert Craven."

"Well, you said something about chemistry, and the chemistry hasn't been there—unless you count hydrogen sulfide with Bert Craven."

"Do you get lonely?"

"Frequently. I'm all right as long as I'm working. Somehow it's worse after I finish a project. I feel let down and empty."

"And you just finished a project."

"Yes, but you're here and I'm having fun."

"I've felt sort of lonely off and on ever since I came up here. I even miss my last girlfriend, Dorothy Minderhout."

"Why do you say 'even'? What was wrong with her?"

"Nothing, really. Chemistry again, I suppose. . . . Her father's an executive with the Hercules Powder Company. That was sort of interesting. She knew all about TNT and stuff like that."

"But she wasn't dynamite?" said Peggy, her lips twitching.

"Ha! No, but she did have an explosive laugh."

"And then came the blowup?"

Vinnie laughed. "Advantage, Singletary!"

They sat for a few moments in mutual pleasure.

"Peggy," said Vinnie, "I think you and I have got a chemical reaction going, so listen . . . do you suppose it'd be possible . . . if, uh, like . . . maybe you and I could sort of, well, get together, if you know what I mean? Pianissimo the loneliness and that let-down empty feeling?"

She smiled. "Not yet."

"Okay, then let's talk about art," he said, covering up briskly. "Those prints in your living room—I saw some of the originals in the Musée d'Orsay in Paris, the one that used to be a train station. That Caillebotte is one of my favorites. . . ."

They talked for an hour about the French Impressionists (Peggy knew far more than he did), and painting, and tile design, and how you know when a tile has baked long enough (there's a peephole in the kiln, though it doesn't let you see much, and little ceramic cones that flop over when the right temperature is reached), and how Peggy used to sit on the grass in Santa Barbara eating her lunch and looking out not only on the Pacific, but also on a national park—the Channel Islands—a perfect spot for whale watching. She asked why Vinnie didn't turn pro after being captain of UCLA's tennis team.

"I'll tell you why. My dad took me down to Rancho La Costa when I was a kid to see Rod Laver play Brian Gottfried, and my god those guys were good! They nearly drove the ball down each other's throat. It was terrifying! No, thanks. Fun, yes, but I never had the killer instinct after that."

Peggy asked if he'd like to see her sketch of the mural she did for Clos d'Ausone. He did. If she had wanted to show him a teddy bear painted on black velvet he would have wanted to see that.

She unrolled a large sheet of paper on the living room floor. Her design was beautiful. Bunches of purple grapes, with green leaves and tendrils, hung on vines at each side, flanking a four-line Latin poem in black lettering:

> *Quis color ille vadis, seras cum propulit*
> *umbras*
> *Hesperus et viridi perfudit monte*
> *Mosellam!*
> *tota natant crispis iuga motibus, et*
> *tremit absens*
> *pampinus, et vitreis vindemia turget in*
> *undis.*

"It's called *Evening on the Moselle*. I have a translation somewhere in my files."

"I had to take Latin at UCLA," said Vinnie, "but Jesus, this is tough stuff! That word order is a killer, but let's see: It talks about Hesperus driving the evening shadows, and color—or something—filling the Moselle with a mountain—a green mountain. I don't know what a *pampinus* is, but there's something about a vineyard seeming to swim in the waves."

"That's about right. Pretty, isn't it?"

"So's your mural. If I ever own the winery, I'll want you to do something for it."

An hour later at the door, Peggy allowed Vinnie to give her a quick kiss on the cheek. This was his big sexy thrill of the evening.

Halfway across the small porch as he left, Vinnie turned and smiled at her.

"Peggy, this evening you said two of the most beautiful words in the English language."

"I did? What are they?"

"Not yet."

ELEVEN

Vinnie went home in the moonlight with a spring in his step and a suffusion of mental moonlight in his head. What a woman that Peggy was! A breeze sprang up as he sauntered down the lane bordering his uncle's vineyard; the fluttering grape leaves shimmered in the moonlight.

When he unlocked the front door of the darkened house, his calico cat shot out and headed for the vineyard. "Good hunting, Ezra!" Vinnie called after him. "Or good potty!"

He was mildly surprised that Uncle Francis wasn't home yet. There must be life in the old boy yet, he thought, being still out on the town; but after all, it was Friday evening.

He faded into sleep as he devised and revised various sexual fantasies, beginning with Peggy's removing the apron, then the blouse (he specified no bra), then, with one of her demure smiles, the skirt—let's see, a lace bikini would be nice. He would be bare chested as they went into a clinch with lots of skin contact. . . . but regrettably he fell asleep before the main event got under way.

His dreams were peaceful and pleasant scenarios of wish fulfillment until the buzzing of the telephone on the nightstand shook him out of them. He picked up the phone, trying to collect his groggy thoughts. He glanced at the red numbers on the digital clock. It was 3:00 in the morning. Uncle Francis, no doubt. Probably his Peugeot had broken down.

He was right, but the breakdown was far more serious than he thought.

"Vincent? This is Holly Shelton. You'd better come down to the St. Helena police station right away."

"What is it? What's happened?"

"It's your uncle. He's been in a terrible car accident—or fire, rather."

"Is he hurt?"

"I'm afraid it's worse than that."

Vinnie was stunned. "You don't mean he's . . . dead?"

"I'm afraid he is. You'd better come down here."

"But—*you're* calling. Are you saying somebody killed him?"

"Come on down and we'll talk about it."

He put on the same clothes he had worn earlier and hurried out to his Mercedes. To his horror, when he turned right at the junction of Zinfandel Lane and Highway 29, he saw a burning red arc of warning flares on the pavement a hundred yards ahead, the flashing yellow lights of a police car—and the blackened hulk of the Peugeot. It seemed to be squatting on the pavement. Even

76

the tires had burned away. A policeman motioned him around the scene and waved him on.

This time he had no trouble finding the St. Helena police station. Sergeant Bailey was behind the desk and nodded grimly when he came in. Detective Shelton was waiting for him. She motioned to a bench at the end of the room.

Seated next to her, his shock and horror starting to give way to grief, Vinnie's eyes shimmered with tears.

"Are you certain it was Uncle Francis?"

"I'm afraid so. But to make sure, we will ask you to go to the morgue in Napa and identify him."

"I can't! I couldn't do it!"

"It's a ghastly formality, I know, but it's necessary. Look, Vincent: You have my deepest sympathy for what you're going through, but it'll help both of us if you can compose yourself. I have a lot of questions and so do you, I imagine. Why don't you take a few minutes."

Vinnie breathed deeply and wiped his eyes with his handkerchief. A thought fleeted through his mind: What's to become of *me?* His emotional storm blotted out any guilt or shame for asking.

"How did it happen? What makes you think somebody killed him?"

"The gas tank exploded."

"Somebody fired a bullet into it? Some religious crazy?"

"No. That only happens on TV. A bullet can't blow up a car."

"What did, then?"

"I think I know. You take a great big gelatin capsule, the kind vets use to shove medicine down a horse's mouth. It's about two and a half or three inches long. You fill it with a common household product you find under the kitchen sink and drop it in the gas tank. There's always a little bit of water at the bottom of a tank, and when the gelatin dissolves, the chemical hits the water and the tank explodes."

"What chemical?"

"Never mind. The fewer people know about it, the better. And I'd rather *you* didn't mention this to anybody because I'll be checking on the qt with all the vets around here. Who do you know that hangs around stables—goes horseback riding?"

"Nobody."

"Where did your uncle go this evening?"

"He went to visit some friends at the Freemark Abbey winery. And then I think he had a date. He was all dressed up."

"Who with?"

"I don't know."

"And you were up at Peggy Singletary's house, right?"

"Yes."

"What time did you leave?"

"About eleven-thirty. Holly, do you think this is connected with the body in the fermentation tank?

"My guess is yes, but we'll see. Has your uncle gotten any threats lately?"

"Not a threat, exactly. A company called Triskelion is trying to buy Château Letessier. They want to build a hotel. An awful guy named Ashton talked to Uncle Francis. He was kind of belligerent, I thought."

"I'm not surprised. You know what a triskelion is? No? It's a three-legged symbol. Among other things it stands for the three-pointed island of Sicily."

"Oh."

"Anybody else?"

"Peggy mentioned 'Doc' Black and Joe Yates."

"They're out of the picture. They left two months ago to work for a winery in the San Joaquin Valley."

"That's all I can think of, unless, well . . ."

"I know what you're thinking. Don't worry, I'll be

checking on a lot of people in and out of the family—ex-wife, ex-employees, any disgruntled employees, and I'll see what I can find out about the Triskelion connection."

"I want to help. I want to nail the bastard that did this. What can I do to help?"

"Stay out of the way and let me do my job."

"No."

"Now look, Vincent!" Holly blew a lock of honey-blond hair away from her eye. "You'll have your hands full trying to run a winery. You are not to run around with a magnifying glass playing amateur sleuth."

"I'm going to talk to people."

Holly reflected a few moments. "All right. I can't very well forbid you to talk to people; but for god's sake don't *interrogate* them. That's *my* job. Okay?"

"Okay."

"You will also report your conversations to me. You are not to go chasing after clues pretending you're Tracer Bullet. Okay?"

"Okay."

"And watch yourself. Keep in mind you may be in danger too."

"Me?"

"What do you think? If this isn't just a revenge murder—if the aim is to ruin Château Letessier—you could be next."

"Oh."

"For starters, you might want to get a gas cap with a lock."

Vinnie gritted his teeth. "I hope whoever it is does try something."

"Let's go down to the morgue now. It'll be better for you to get the miserable part of this over and done with."

Following Detective Shelton as they left the police station, Vinnie sensed a powerful change in himself.

He had acquired the killer instinct.

TWELVE

T he corpse of Uncle Francis, in the pugilistic stance of a fire victim, was blackened, charred, and carbonized like burned meat on a barbecue grill. Vinnie could bear to look at it for only a few seconds; he turned away, on the verge of vomiting, but identified it as his uncle even though he could not recognize him. Detective Shelton signed the death certificate as deputy coroner.

Vinnie endured that night and the following week by lapsing into a strange mixture of numbness and hypertension that crowded out his killer instinct for the time being. Sheer necessity forced him to perform tasks and go through formalities that were foreign to his nature. The worst were making funeral arrangements and visiting

Uncle Francis's lawyer in St. Helena, where he got no joy from learning that Francis had indeed willed the winery and most of his estate to Vinnie, and had taken the precaution of giving him a power of attorney.

His uncle had left no instructions about his preferences regarding a funeral, but from the very few comments Francis had ever made about religion, Vinnie got the impression that his uncle was either a lapsed Catholic or a fallen-away Catholic. Francis hadn't been to mass in so long that once, he said, attending a funeral at St. Helena Catholic on a hot summer day, he looked around for a paper cup in the vestibule so he could get a drink of water—from the holy water font, until someone pointed out the black cross painted on it. Vinnie decided the church was worth a try.

Father Annino, after expressing his heartfelt sympathy, was somewhat amused at Vinnie's asking whether his uncle could be buried in consecrated ground even though the man hadn't been to confession in ten years.

"Of course," he said, tapping the ash off his cigarette. "The only thing I couldn't do is give him a final blessing."

"How about last rites?"

"That's only for the gravely ill. I'm sorry I was unable to do that for your uncle. . . . I gather you're not in the faith yourself. Too bad, with a name like Vincent. St. Vincent is the patron saint of vintners."

"No, my father became a Presbyterian, so I did too—for a while."

"A while? What happened?"

"I won a Sunday school prize, and when I walked up to the pulpit to get it, the minister handed me a brand-new hymnbook."

"That was the prize?"

"That was it. It made both my father and me so mad we quit the church."

"Those dumb Protestants! If that had been a Catholic

church, they would have given you a bat and a ball and you'd *still* be going!''

The church was crowded for the funeral mass. All the workers from Château Letessier were there, members of the Napa Valley Vintners Association and the County Board of Supervisors, and numerous personal friends. Accompanied by George Preston, Adrienne Letessier appeared, exposing enough décolleté to make a baby cry. Bert Craven and Delphine sat in the family pew with Vinnie. Peggy Singletary sat in the pew just behind him and gave him a comforting pat or two on the shoulder.

Vinnie suffered numbly through the Mass and the singing of Dies Irae and the Te Deum, and endured the burial with the stupor of a somnabulist.

When it was over, Bert Craven approached him and said quietly, ''This may sound a little out of line right now, but I know you're in a jam, so I'm willing to come in and take over your books for you. Just say the word.''

''Thanks, Bert, but Uncle Francis advised me not to go into business with a relative or friend. I think he's right.''

''At a time like this he could be wrong.''

''Maybe. But no. Thanks for the offer, anyway.''

''Okay, it's your funeral. Oh, sorry about that.'' He walked away.

Peggy joined Vinnie and put her arm through his. ''Would you like to come to my house for a while?''

''Peggy, I am so wrung out I can't do anything but sleep.''

''Come have dinner, then, when you wake up. Just give me a call.''

''Okay, but don't expect a laff riot for young and old alike.''

THIRTEEN

He slept till dusk and then trudged up to Peggy's house. She gave him a boccie ball with two jiggers of amaretto, and they sat exchanging the conventional remarks of mourners.

"May I say I'm glad you're here?" said Vinnie, finally.

"You may. That goes for me too."

"And thanks for not trying to 'cheer me up.' "

"You're entitled to feel depressed."

"I don't know about 'depressed.' Exhausted, maybe."

"You seem depressed to me. And the first thing I learned in analysis was that depression is anger turned inward on yourself. Do you feel any anger?"

"You bet I do. For the first time in my life I feel like a killer! If I find out who killed Uncle Francis I want to kill him! And if Holly finds out, I hope I have a chance to get at him myself!"

Peggy made no pious remarks about leaving it up to the courts.

"Good for you. That's better than depression. Maybe before long you'll be your lighthearted self again. I hope so."

"So do I."

At the door, when Peggy kissed him full on the lips, he felt a faint stirring of lightheartedness. In any event, as he walked off down the road, he was a more complex man than he had been a few days before.

He arose the next morning in a state of apprehension, because he was now the master of the winery and he had no idea how to go about it. Run a *winery?* He felt as he did once when three of his fraternity brothers insisted he learn to play pinochle, which he didn't want to do. They sat him down, dealt out the cards, turned to Vinnie and said, "All right—meld." He blew up and left the table.

Mrs. Barton, puffy-eyed from weeping, served him a breakfast of ham and eggs, toast, and biscuits with honey, and insisted he eat it. "You haven't been eating enough to keep a sparrow alive," she said. "Now you eat what's put before you, or you and I are going to lock horns!"

"All right. Thanks, Mrs. Barton."

She watched him to make sure he followed orders, but he was sunk in thought.

"Mrs. Barton, what in *hell* am I going to do?"

"Hush up. You'll do fine. And leave out the 'hell.' It says in Scripture that every foolish word will be accounted for."

"But I don't know anything about running a business. I even dropped out of financial math when I was in school."

"You can't do any worse than that George Preston—and I know whereof I speak! Instead of making money for this place all he ever thought about was cutting expenses. He even wanted to cut *my* salary. The man was tight as Dick's hatband. And that Adrienne was another one. We're lucky to be shut of those two."

"They are quite a pair, aren't they?"

"She's a hussy, that's all there is to it. The way she dressed! For a while there she took to wearing purple lipstick. I came in on her once when she had her lips all pooched out and was putting it on and I said, 'I declare, Adrienne, your mouth looks like a jaybird's ass at pokeberry time.' She didn't like it, but it's the truth that hurts."

Vinnie had to smile. "You've got her number all right—but what about those foolish words you just mentioned?"

"I know; sometimes my feelings get the better of me."

Vinnie pleased her—and himself, he found—by finishing his breakfast. He sat wondering what to do next, and then remembered his uncle's instructions. He went down to the bottling room, where Gil Fernandez had resumed bottling the rest of the '88 cabernet sauvignon.

Vinnie had passed through the bottling room months before, but he remembered only that it was full of complex Rube Goldberg machinery circling around, performing a series of bewildering operations ("Operator presses Button A, causing Wine B to pour into Bottle C, triggering Piston D to come down on Lead Foil E and Cork F . . ."), all this at a rate of fifty-five bottles a minute.

Gil Fernandez, every gleaming black hair in place, was operating the machine with the nonchalance of someone driving a car. Behind him three women in white cotton blouses stood at a bench gluing labels on the bottles.

"Hi, Vinnie!"

"Hi, Gil. Can I talk to you for a minute?"

"You're the boss," he replied with a grin. He turned the machine off. "Fantastic contraption, ain't it? Now if we can just sell this stuff. . . . okay, what's up?"

"I'd like you to be the new resident manager."

Gil's eyes widened and he rubbed his nose. "Well, that's a showstopper! You mean that?"

"Certainly. It was one of my uncle's last wishes."

"No fooling! Why, sure—you're on!"

"One thing, though: Will you go on doing the pruning or at least supervise it? Or is that something resident managers do?"

"*This* one will."

"Great. At least we'll have one guy around here who knows what he's doing."

"Hey, don't worry, Vinnie. You'll catch on. A lot of jobs are kind of obvious when they come up—like bottling."

"Yeah, and like meeting the payroll. When *is* the next payday?"

"October first."

"Wonderful. I need my fifty bucks. I suppose you'll get the same pay George Preston was getting, whatever that was. Maybe more—assuming the money's there."

"Fine."

"How was Preston as manager?"

"Efficient, I'll say that for him. Efficient but highhanded. Kept pretty much to himself and treated the rest of us like peons, including me—*and* Francis. He acted like he was king and your uncle was just the treasurer. He thought Francis was a good wine maker but a lousy manager."

"I've heard that one before."

"We had a hell of a fistfight once—did your uncle tell you about it?"

"No. What was it about?"

"We got into an argument over something, I don't remember what, and he called me a greaser so I called him a *pendejo.*"

"What's a *pendejo?*"

"Can be 'nerd,' can be something a lot worse. But 'greaser'? Okay, I started out as a Mexican-American; then I became a Chicano; then I was Hispanic; now I'm Latino. They're all okay with me, but call me 'spick' or 'greaser' and sorry, I have to put up my fists, so I went at him even though he's bigger and tougher and stronger than me. He connected with a lot of roundhouse rights while I hit him with two hundred jabs. By the time your uncle broke it up, I was bludgeoned and he was pulverized. Best fight I've had since the one Holly arrested me for."

"Did you know about him and Adrienne while he was here?"

"Everybody did. You know, it was a funny thing. Preston and Nilla Toscana down at the bank used to be a really hot item around here. He even dated her now and then *after* he hooked up with Adrienne. It was like he was trying to make up his mind."

"Choosing between lobster and caviar, you might say."

Gil laughed. "That about covers it. Both of them tasty dishes. But if I know George, he saw richer prospects with Adrienne, and he was right. They sure took Francis to the cleaners, didn't they?"

"So my uncle said. Well, Gil, go ahead and take over as resident manager, whatever that involves—unless you'd like to trade places with me."

"No, thanks! My dad used to have a sign in his shop that said 'Work hard eight hours a day and don't worry, and eventually you'll be boss and work twelve hours a day and have all the worry.' So—you're the boss, and good luck."

"Thanks a lot. Okay, finish your bottling, I guess. . . . Say, I meant to ask: How come all the bottles come to you upside down?"

"They've been sterilized, and then the machine gives them a puff of nitrogen to keep the oxygen out."

"And you put them in the cases upside down to keep the corks wet?"

"Yep. And keep oxygen out."

"Makes sense. All right, I'll let you go while I figure out what *I'm* going to do next."

Up at the house, sitting in Francis's office, Vinnie realized he had to start thinking about money and debts and payrolls. His stomach clenched just looking at his uncle's row of three-drawer file cabinets full of records. He wished once more that he had taken a few business courses, and that he hadn't dropped out of financial math. In his defense, one reason he dropped out—aside from a looming *F*—was that the professor was a half-senile old guy who kept working problems wrong on the blackboard, rubbing them out with his hand, and then rubbing his head and his suit lapels. By the end of the hour he looked like Frosty the Snowman. Vinnie gave up.

As he was trying to prod himself into opening the files, the phone rang. It was Detective Shelton.

"Interim report, Vinnie, about the body of Richard Mifflin. I'm positive a clerk at the Vacaville prison loading dock took a bribe to give it to somebody. It had to be either him or somebody at the San Francisco end, and somehow I can't see an employee of a busy and prestigious hospital pulling such a stunt. Nor can I imagine our practical joker managing to arrange things at the San Francisco end and then driving from there across the Golden Gate Bridge all the way to Vallejo and up to Napa. Too complicated and too risky. The simplest answer is Vacaville and side roads."

"Have you talked to the guy?"

"Yes. His name is Lester Shira, and he's stonewalling—for good reason, naturally. He has a signed receipt for the body from a man claiming to be from the hospital medical school—says he had no reason to doubt he was bona fide. 'Besides,' he says, 'who'd want a jailbird's stiff?' "

"Who signed the receipt?"

"It was signed 'Peter O'Toole.' "

"Oh, clever. Did he say what the man looked like?"

"Middle-aged, average height, no distinguishing features. The man signed the receipt, loaded the body in what at least appeared to be an ambulance, and off he went. The clerk isn't sure he'd recognize him again: 'You know how they come and go,' he said. I'll keep working on that angle."

"How about my uncle?"

"I'm checking gas stations, trying to find out when your uncle last had a fill up. I think it took a full tank of gas to produce an explosion like that. How about you? Have you been talking to people?"

"No. I can't even start yet. Right now I've got to think about money. But thanks for all you're doing."

"My job."

Vinnie went back to the files. He managed to find folders labeled "Bank Loans," "Accounts Payable," and "Payroll," and found his uncle's checkbook in the middle desk drawer. The bank balance had been kept up to date, so at least he could read that. An AT&T 6610 typewriter stood on the desk, as did a new Macintosh Classic computer with a hard disk. He turned it on, selected the hard-disk icon, and found similar file names. He guessed that Uncle Francis was in the middle of computerizing his operation.

Alternating between the file folders and the computer, at the cost of a throbbing head, Vinnie jotted down some of the important numbers that leapt out at him, and got the appalling impression that after the payroll was taken care of, Château Letessier needed some four hundred thirty-seven thousand dollars, and needed it right away. But that sounded sky-high, and given his shaky grasp of arithmetic, he concluded that he'd better call in an accountant. But whom? It struck him as unwise to call someone he didn't know, who might leak information about the winery's financial state. Reluctantly, he thought of Bert Craven, and reluctantly phoned him.

Bert was only too glad to come have a look, for a fee. He whipped through the files and called up computer programs Vinnie didn't know were there, made rapid notes with pencil and pad, and crunched numbers on a calculator. When he finished he gave Vinnie a look he seemed to have a talent for: mixed amusement and scorn.

"It's bad, but nowhere near as bad as you thought. Where you got that four-hundred thousand figure I will never know. For right now—and I mean *right now*—you need to send checks totaling twelve hundred some-odd dollars that Francis still owed on oak barrels and the bottling machine."

"I can handle that."

"I don't see how, unless you've been embezzling."

Vinnie kept quiet about Uncle Francis's sub-rosa account in Vallejo.

"Don't worry, I can handle it."

Bert lifted both hands. "All *right,* if you say so. Up to *you.* But pay those. It would be terrible PR for the winery if you didn't. *However:* Once you've met the payroll—about thirty thousand—you won't have enough for the loan payment to the Vintners Bank, and Francis has already been charged heavy penalties for falling behind on *that* for a few months. In about two shakes they're going to find him—you—in default and you *will* have to sell off some acreage that served as collateral—not too *tough* because there are people willing to *buy.*"

"Such as Triskelion."

"So you were listening after all. The trouble is, even if you get an extension or refinance or whatever, you'll be right back on square one. You don't have any working capital! You need another two hundred thousand cash just to keep going—two-fifty or three hundred to be safe."

"Where am I going to get that kind of money? Beg it from the bank?"

"No, no, don't beg. If it was me, I'd go on the offensive—sock it to 'em. I'd tell them they should give it to me to protect their investment."

"I'm not you, but I'll try it."

"One thing I don't understand, though: I see no sign of business-interruption insurance backing up that loan. You know what that is? It covers loss of business income."

"Uncle Francis said he let his insurance lapse."

"He must have meant some other kind, not this. There never *was* a business-interruption policy, and I'm amazed the bank didn't require one. Somebody fucked up royally. Maybe they didn't know how; it takes a sophisticated broker to write one. But that's no excuse—somebody really screwed up. Howsoever, you're back in the bind Francis was in, so take your choice: Sell some acreage or try the bank."

"Maybe you could talk to them. You said you have bank connections."

"Not with Vintners. Sorry, you're on your own. Take my advice and get down there today."

Bert departed with a hundred and fifty-dollar fee, leaving Vinnie facing another challenge totally foreign to his experience: trying to renegotiate a two-hundred fifty thousand dollar loan.

He edged into the Vintners Bank on Main Street and looked around at the tellers' windows and lines of customers and bank officers sitting at desks in the carpeted area. One of them was the terrific-looking chick he noticed earlier in the summer when he came in with Uncle

Francis. He saw her later, once, in the front yard of her house near Madrona and Main. Now that he had a better look he saw she was more than terrific, she was a knockout. She had black hair, full on the crown, short at the neck, flawless ivory skin, Mediterranean blue eyes. Her bright red lips matched the red of her jacket, under which she wore a frilly white blouse. Her skirt was black-and-white checked. The total effect was that of a self-assured, dynamic professional woman.

She was talking on the telephone and manipulating a yellow pencil with her fingers. He edged close enough to see her nameplate: NILLA TOSCANA. The one Peggy said Bert Craven had pawed at a winery party. Italian, not Greek. Below her name was her job title: CHIEF LOAN OFFI-CER. His nervousness subsided into relief. He had expected a beady-eyed fat guy with two thumbs in his vest, chomping a cigar. This was more like it—the gentle sex, the sympathetic woman. He approached her desk. She hung up the phone and gave Vinnie a bright professional smile.

"Yes, can I help you, Mr. Letessier?"

"You know who I am."

"Of course. You must be here about the loan."

"Right."

So far, so good.

She moved a vase of red roses to the end of her desk to clear their view. Vinnie noted a card attached to the bouquet reading, "Affectueusement, André." *Lacroix?* Almost had to be, he thought, although the supervisor must be in his sixties now if he had been in the French Resistance. The sixties weren't all that old these days, of course, but still, it seemed an odd December-May connection.

"Let's see where we stand," said Nilla, turning to her computer. She did little more than glance briefly at the screen when the loan record came up. "And where we stand doesn't look too good, Mr. Letessier, to be honest

94

with you. I hope you've come in to make a payment—
hopefully a double payment?"

"No. In fact, I'd like to get an extension, a couple of
months maybe, till we can get caught up."

"Your uncle already had two extensions. By the way,
I'm terribly sorry about what happened." She compressed her lips for a moment to show she was terribly
sorry. "But under the circumstances I'm afraid an extension is impossible." She gave him a pleasant smile.

"Then what you should do is add another two-hundred thousand to the loan."

"Why should I do that?" Another pleasant smile.

"To protect your investment. And think of all the
legal complications you'd avoid if you had to foreclose or
whatever you do."

That amused her. "We're quite competent to handle
legal complications."

"But what's the worry? The winery has plenty of
assets to back up the loan."

"That's why we made the loan. And why we're not
worried."

"It wouldn't bother you if Château Letessier went out
of business?"

"It's happened many times before." Her phone rang.
"Will you excuse me?"

While she talked on the phone, Vinnie's gaze wan-
dered around the bank, back to Nilla Toscana's alabaster
desk set, to the roses, to a half-eaten carob candy bar on
the desk, to her in basket, where he was startled to recognize the return address on an envelope. It was from the
headquarters of Triskelion Enterprises in The Lakes,
Nevada. Nilla Toscana's address was typewritten, not
computerized or run off on an Avery label.

In his mind's eye, a cluster of four names came
together: André Lacroix, Bert Craven, and Triskelion
(Ashton?), each with a line drawn to Nilla Toscana at the

center. Quite a popular woman, who seemed to do far more than mix business with pleasure—she pureed them.

"Sorry for the interruption," said Nilla, hanging up. "Now—where were we?"

"I was asking you to renegotiate or refinance the loan—or maybe just let me make the interest payments for a couple of months until things straighten out."

"Out of the question. We've been too lenient already. And things clearly are not going to 'straighten out.'"

"What makes you so sure?"

"May I be brutally frank? I understand you have a degree in French, which hardly prepares you for running a winery, does it? In short, we at the bank see you as hopelessly incompetent." Bright smile.

"I'm learning fast."

"Not fast enough, so the answer is no deal. So *if* you will excuse me—Mr. Letessier?" She picked up some papers and tapped them on their edges like a TV newscaster at program's end.

Vinnie rose and stood there for several moments, watching her with curiosity.

Nilla returned his gaze. "Something more to say?"

"Two things. Speaking of incompetence, how come you neglected to make Uncle Francis take out a business-interruption policy? Your superiors might frown on that—if they learn about it."

Nilla seemed caught off base for a second or two. "And your second thing?"

"I've had a new experience. You're the first female prick I ever met."

Far from being enraged, Nilla's eyes sparkled. She looked . . . triumphant.

Vinnie, however, walked out feeling angry and humiliated. Out on the sidewalk he paused, thinking, and decided on two courses of action. First, he would follow another piece of advice Uncle Francis had given him: If you need money and don't have it, find somebody who does have it. Second, he would call on André Lacroix and find out how he fit into the scheme of things. And "scheme" appeared to be the right word.

FOURTEEN

Vinnie remembered Uncle Francis mentioning that his student intern came from a rich and aristocratic Armenian family. He couldn't remember the name, but he remembered "rich" well enough, and the young intern by definition was interested in viticulture. It was worth a try.

But what in hell was that name? Gitche Gumee? Kitchy Koochy? Tutti Frutti? It was no use. Vinnie gave up and resigned himself to flipping through the cards in his uncle's Rolodex file, hoping he'd recognize the name. He lucked out at once, toward the end of the *A*'s. There it was: Arshagouni, Dikran, with a phone number and address over in Modesto, in the San Joaquin Valley below Stockton. Neither name sounded Armenian to Vinnie, but for all he cared it could have been Swahili or Twi. He dialed the number.

Mrs. Arshagouni answered and was happy to call her son to the phone. Dikran knew all about what had happened to Francis, and said the loss cut him to the quick. "What a man he was! That summer I spent with him was worth a whole year at UC Davis. He had a wire edge to him, all right, but he treated me like a junior partner instead of a lowly intern. And what can I do for you?"

"You just put your finger on it."

"I don't follow you."

"How would you like to *be* a junior partner? Or partner?"

"Are you serious?"

"Sure. If you have a lot of money. Do you have a lot of money?"

Dikran laughed. "Well! You don't fool around, do you?"

"Not in the fix I'm in, I don't."

"Then I won't either. The answer is no, I don't, but my father is loaded. You want me to buy in on Château Letessier?"

"Yeah."

"For how much?"

"I don't know. I'm no good with figures."

"Make a guess."

"Okay." Vinnie swallowed and worked up his nerve. "How does half a million sound?"

"Plausible. That's for a full partnership?"

"Sure. Think you can swing it?"

"Probably. My father would just as soon get me out of here because I'm interested in wine making and he raises melons. Melons, Mr. Letessier—"

"Vinnie."

"Melons, Vinnie, leave me cold—figuratively speaking, that is, because summers in Modesto are hot as the

100

hinges of hell and three whores' hearts. I have grown to detest everything starting with a *C:* casabas, cantaloupes, crenshaws, cucumbers, carrots. Chardonnay and chocolate are okay, of course. So I'll take Napa any day, and my three brothers can keep their casabas. Why don't I come talk it over with you tomorrow morning? And meanwhile I'll see what my father says."

"Great! If you can swing this, Dikran—"

"Make it Dik, with no 'c'."

"If this works out, Dik, you will frankly be saving my ass. We've got problems here. So hell—go ahead. Take advantage of me. I invite you. Do anything you want. Rename the place after yourself."

"I don't think the world is ready for an Armenian winery," Dik said, laughing. " 'Château Arshagouni'? No, the name lacks that certain something. But let's not jump the gun, count our chickens, or cross our bridges, and we'll talk it over tomorrow. How does eleven o'clock sound?"

"Wonderful. See you then."

Vinnie hung up the phone feeling a surge of relief and optimism. Dik Arshagouni sounded like a neat guy. He looked forward to seeing him.

Ezra the cat strolled in, went to the sliding glass door without looking at Vinnie, and sat down, waiting to be let out. Someone once told Vinnie that a male calico cat would be worth five hundred dollars. Ezra behaved as if that was a ridiculously low estimate. Vinnie slid the door open a foot. Ezra rose and took his time sniffing the track, the jamb, the edge of the door.

"Ezra," said Vinnie, "I want to know. What is it you cats get out of sniffing aluminum?"

Ezra gave him a bland look, moved halfway out the door, and stopped.

"And why must you always be *in utrumque paratus,* for Pete's sake?"

Ezra didn't know Latin.

"It means 'ready either way,' dummy. It's the title of a poem by Clough."

Ezra didn't know Clough either, and didn't care. He eased out.

Vinnie got on the phone again and called André Lacroix's office. After a short wait, his secretary responded that the supervisor would be delighted to see Vinnie at 2:30 that afternoon.

Vinnie drove his red Mercedes down to the Civic Center in Napa. From the looks of the buildings, it seemed to him that the architects had gotten their blueprints mixed up. The Hall of Justice, where Holly Shelton worked, looked like a library. The Napa library looked like a jail. Jail inmates were mowing the lawn and raking leaves in front of the County Administration Building at Third and Coombs, where the Board of Supervisors met. It was an attractive building with an entrance resembling a grape arbor. A plaque cemented to the wall bore the county emblem, bunches of grapes suspended above vineyards, emphasizing the agricultural strength of the Napa Valley, and its commitment to the wine industry. Uncle Francis told Vinnie it hadn't always been that way. Not at all. Back in the 1960s there had been a terrible fight among winegrowers, table grape growers, and people who wanted to develop the valley into a bedroom community for San Francisco. It almost came to outright violence, but the grapes won out.

Vinnie entered the lobby and took the elevator to Lacroix's third-floor office, representing District 2.

Lacroix came out from his desk and welcomed Vinnie with a handshake and greeting. The man looked as if he had spent more time on the beaches of Santa Monica than in Napa. He was brown as pork gravy, balding, slim, wiry, about 5'7, with alert brown eyes.

Vinnie returned his greeting by saying, *"Bonjour, Monsieur Lacroix,"* and then commenting, *"On dit que vous venez de Bordeaux."*

Lacroix raised his eyebrows in surprise.

"Comment allez-vous aujourd'hui?" Vinnie asked.

"Je me défends," Lacroix replied, with a wide smile. *"Et vous?"*

They proceeded to chat in French for a minute or two, during which Lacroix surprised Vinnie by referring to wine as *lu vin* instead of *le vin.*

"You sound more as if you come from Limousin, Mr. Lacroix," said Vinnie, still in French.

"Shh, that's a secret!" Lacroix replied in English. "I was born there, but Bordeaux became my real hometown, and Bordeaux is better PR in Napa at election time. But hey, what say we can the Frog chatter and talk plain USA, all right?"

"Fine with me."

"Sit down. Take the sofa. How about some coffee?"

Lacroix poured two cups from a carafe and seated himself in an armchair. "That was a terrible, terrible tragedy, what happened to your uncle. Believe me, we'll miss him sorely around here, everybody will miss him; he helped pioneer the Napa wine industry back in the sixties, you know. Jeez, I hate going to the funerals of old friends like that. Francis and I had our differences, as who doesn't with a politician, but we were friends anyway."

"Yes, Uncle Francis spoke of you—warmly."

"I'm glad to hear that. Okay—tell me what I can do you for, but I think I can guess. Along with the winery you inherited all of Francis's problems."

"That's for sure. They were bad enough before he was murdered and before that dead body showed up in the tank."

"What about that stiff? They ever find out where it came from?"

An oddly put question. Mifflin's name hadn't been revealed; as far as the public knew, he had been killed at the winery and shoved into the tank. But perhaps Vinnie was reading too much into so ambiguous a term as "came from."

"No. They're still working on it."

" 'Working on it.' Our local boys in blue are pretty good with the rural stuff, but something like this may be beyond them. They ought to call in the FBI."

"It isn't a federal case."

"Yes, but who knows? Maybe the guy's civil rights were violated, especially if he's Mexican. Was he Mexican?"

"No, Anglo."

"Well, let's get back to our sheep, as the old play says. Tell me why you're here."

"Mostly to educate myself—sort of get the lay of the land. I've heard a lot of talk lately about tourism versus winegrowing, and you must be an expert on that."

"As the GI's used to say, you ain't just muttering through pursed lips, Mac. It's a running battle; keeps us supervisors on the hot seat all the time, trying to maintain a balance. And you know what? With every decision we make, some people get mad as hell. We promote tourism—a major industry in Napa—and the winegrowers start yelling about 'crows.' Decide in favor of the growers, and business people claim we're against progress. You can't win."

"I'm in sort of a bind like that myself. A company in Nevada wants to buy Château Letessier and set up a combination hotel and vineyard."

"Do you plan to sell?"

"I don't know yet."

"It would be an easy out for you."

"Sure, but the idea of a hotel—Uncle Francis would spin in his grave."

"Up to you."

"Up to you too, isn't it? Let me ask you: Have you ever heard of an outfit called Triskelion Enterprises?"

"Nope. New one on me."

"They're the ones so eager to buy. My question is, even if I decide to sell, what are the chances that the Board of Supervisors and the Planning Commission would okay a hotel?"

"Offhand, I'd say we'd be against it unless they put up a hell of a convincing case; but if it *was* a convincing case, then it'd be . . . a convincing case. So it all depends."

"It also depends on whether I can get my hands on some money. I tried the bank, but the loan officer down there gave me a really rough time, a woman named Nilla Toscana. Do you know her?"

"Nilla? Oh sure, I run into her now and then. What a babe, right? Like the GI's used to say, man, I could eat that with a mess-kit spoon!" Lacroix laughed. "Pardon the language. Thank god we're among friends."

"You sure picked up a lot of GI slang in Bordeaux."

"No—Lyons, mostly, where I was liberated. Hey, I know I overdo it sometimes, but you can't imagine what a goddamn thrill it was when the Americans came in. Every one of those guys was like a god to me. They got there just in time too. I was in the Resistance, you know, and the Gestapo finally caught up with me."

"What did you do in the Resistance?"

"Radio operator in Libourne, on the Dordogne River near Bordeaux. I used to broadcast information to London from a bedroom window while the Gestapo roamed around in electronic trucks trying to locate me by triangulation. They finally did it while I was sending a long message. There was an armoire in the bedroom with a false bottom, and I was trying to hide my transmitter in it when I heard the front door bust open. Man, I didn't know whether to shit or go blind, so I closed one eye and farted."

Lacroix laughed at the memory. "They took me in and beat me up pretty bad, but that night I escaped through a window no more than a foot wide and made it to Lyons. They caught me again in Lyons, this time with a set of crystals in my pocket, but the Americans came in and it was the krauts' turn to run."

"Saved by the bell."

"Of course I did other things," Lacroix went on, warming to his story. "Cutting telephone wires. Sabotage. Hey—want to know how to make a simple time bomb? You light a cigarette, tuck it under the flap of a folder of matches, and toss it into a passing freight train. When the cigarette burns down to the match heads you're three miles away, and if you're in luck the *boches* have lost a carload of whatever."

Vinnie was rather disappointed to hear this. Lacroix surely wouldn't be telling such a thing if he had anything to do with Uncle Francis's murder. On the other hand he agreed with Peggy Singletary: Lacroix seemed almost too good to be true. And behind the man's jauntiness and ready smile, Vinnie sensed a vague hint of the *salaud*, to use Francis's epithet. Maybe it was the small white lies, or maybe the constant display of too many teeth in that brown face. The most trivial impressions sometimes turn people off. He remembered that his mother wouldn't vote for Pat Brown, Senior, as governor of California because "he always looked like he was smelling something bad."

Leaving the building, he decided to check up on Lacroix. He returned to St. Helena and stopped at the offices of the *St. Helena Star* on Main Street. He soon found two major articles about him, the first appearing in 1964 when Lacroix, "a hero of the French Resistance," arrived in Napa and opened a radio and electronics store, and the other in 1980, when he was elected to his first four-year term on the five-member Board of Supervisors. His photograph accompanied each article; aside from boasting more hair in the first one, he seemed to have changed but little over the years. For a small fee the newspaper was happy to photocopy the earlier one and supply the later one out of their files.

Back at the winery, Vinnie phoned the French National Tourist Office in San Francisco, and got the address of a museum in Bordeaux that preserved a body of documents on World War II from 1939 to 1945, including a wealth of materials on the French Resistance. He sat down at his uncle's AT&T typewriter and proceeded to compose a letter—the first, he realized, that he had ever written in French:

Musée Jean Moulin,
Place Jean Moulin,
33000 Bordeaux,
FRANCE

Monsieur le Directeur,

Je me permets de m'adresser à vous pour une complaisance . . . I would much appreciate your sending me any information you might have concerning a certain ANDRÉ GHISLAIN LACROIX . . . who purports to be a veteran of the French Resistance as a member of *Ceux de la Libération* and is now an American citizen serving on the Napa County, California, Board of Supervisors. He informs me that from 1943 to 1945 he served as a radio operator for the Resistance in Libourne and was arrested twice by the Gestapo, once in Bordeaux and once in Lyons. I enclose two photos of Lacroix taken in 1964 and 1980. I realize that this is scanty information to go on, but . . . [etc., etc.].
En vous remerciant, je vous prie d'agréer, Monsieur, mes salutations empressées,

Vincent Letessier

He affixed a fifty-cent stamp to the envelope and put it in the outgoing mail.

FIFTEEN

Dikran Arshagouni arrived at the winery promptly at 11:00 the next morning, bringing a young woman with him. Vinnie opened the sliding door to the dining room, and he and Peggy stepped out onto the patio to greet them. Watching them as they came up the walk, Vinnie felt sure that if they appeared on an Armenian travel poster, people would rush to book flights to Yerevan.

Dikran had black hair and brown eyes, but his complexion was so fair that Vinnie had to junk any ideas he had about the "typical" Armenian. At 5'9, Dikran was shorter than Vinnie and more sturdily built. He was wearing a blue ultra-suede jacket, gray slacks, and a white cotton shirt open at the collar.

The young woman with him was a petite and pretty 5'2, wearing a short-skirted, ivory-linen dress shot with gold threads. She looked—well, more typically Armenian, with her tan complexion and curly brown hair. She had large, liquid, brown eyes, Bambi eyes, slanted slightly upward, with long black eyelashes, but she soon proved to be neither Bambi nor bimbo. Near her mouth was a beauty spot, a dark dot that must have invited Dikran to "kiss here."

They all shook hands and made their introductions.

"My fiancée, Satenig Najarian," said Dik, "better known as Sandy."

Vinnie introduced his "friend," Peggy Singletary. Dik and Sandy looked at her approvingly.

"Close friend?" said Dik, with a hopeful eye.

"Ask Peggy."

"Very close," said Peggy, smiling, "but friends."

"Do you live here?" Sandy asked.

"No, I have my own place up the road. I'm a custom-tile designer."

"I'm a writer-editor," said Sandy. "At least I was. I'm marrying Dik just in time, because I quit my last two jobs."

"Because of trouble, or to get married?"

"Trouble. I worked on a trade paper for an oil company, until they laid plans to drill a lot of wells off the California coast; I got mad and went to work for a big lumber company. *They* wanted me to write articles on what a great idea it was to saw down all the seventeen-hundred-year-old redwoods up in Del Norte and Humboldt Counties."

"They wanted more than that," said Dikran. "Tell 'em the funny office joke."

"Oh, that—what my boss said. 'A secretary,' he said—ha, ha—'can't be considered a permanent fixture in the office until she's been screwed on the desk.' 'And a boss can't be defined as a boss,' I said, 'until he has a rounded protuberance on his head.' He got mad, I got mad, and I quit."

"So welcome to Napa County," said Vinnie, "where people want to develop the land all up and down both sides of Highway Twenty-nine—and build a hotel in this vineyard."

"Outrageous!" said Sandy. "Don't let them do it."

"That's why Dik is here, I hope," said Vinnie. "Let's go in and talk about it."

"Fine," said Dik. "And to quote the great Robert Benchley, let's all get together and make this the best year the Armenians ever had."

Over a lunch that began with Belgian endive, cream cheese, and golden caviar, along with a bottle of sauvignon blanc, followed by scallops with a cream sauce served on scallop shells, enhanced by a bottle of chardonnay, Dik and Vinnie reviewed the winery's problems and settled on the terms of their new partnership. Both of them were enthusiastic about the prospects for Château Letessier, partly because of the new infusion of money, and partly because of the excellence of the two proprietary wines they were enjoying.

"Not only that," said Dik, "from what you tell me, you—we—have eight acres of gewürztraminer still on the vines, which means not only a late harvest, but still better, these grapes have botrytis—noble rot."

"I've never understood how that works," said Peggy.

"It's a benign fungus that gets on the grapes," said Dik, "and sucks water out, leaving a high sugar content inside. Makes a terrific dessert wine that should sell for twenty-five dollars a half-bottle."

"If we can sell it," said Vinnie.

"We'll sell it. We'll sell it if we have to come out and *call* it full-bodied!"

They agreed that Vinnie would retain a 51 percent

interest in the winery and Dik 49, Gil Fernandez would be resident manager, Dik would handle finances and act as wine maker, and Vinnie would have the right of final approval of Dik's wine, this last being based on two considerations: Though Vinnie was not a wine maker he had a connoisseur's taste, and he insisted that they perpetuate Uncle Francis's high standards of quality.

"Okay, with two small exceptions," said Dik. "First, aging cabernet four years is swell if you're filthy rich and just having fun, but in view of our present problems I'd say we age it three years max. Second, Francis's prejudice against merlot was really unreasonable. Merlot's a soft wine that makes cabernet mature sooner. Besides, you know what the most expensive Bordeaux wine is?"

"Château Pétrus."

"Right. And Pétrus is ninety-five percent merlot."

"All right, I'll go along with that—but geez, have you met Bert Craven? He made the same two points, and it gets right in amongst me to think a guy like that could be right."

"I've met him and I don't like him."

"I don't either," said Vinnie. "Money is the only thing in the world he's interested in. He doesn't give a damn about quality or about wine as wine."

"There's an old Armenian proverb, Vinnie: 'Pigs never see the stars.' "

"That fits Bert, all right. Oh, one other thing: I got another phone call yesterday from Roy Ashton, that guy I told you about at Triskelion Enterprises, the outfit that wants to buy the winery."

"Tell him to go piss up a rope."

"I sort of did. I told him he was too late. But then I believe the guy actually threatened me."

"What did he say?"

"He got insistent. He said if I 'knew what was good

for me' I'd give serious thought to their proposition. He wants to come see me tomorrow at ten-thirty."

Dik tapped his teeth with a fingernail. "Let him come. I've got a terrific idea how we can handle him."

SIXTEEN

Dikran showed up the next day with his brothers Krikor, Aram, and Mourad. All three were taller and darker than Dik, with bushy but neatly styled black hair. When their sense of humor didn't get the better of them, Aram and Mourad looked menacing, with buccaneers' mustaches that drooped at the ends. Krikor could look equally menacing clean shaven. The result was that although they wore Giorgio Armani jackets, Hermès neckties, and Bally moccasins, they could have passed for fighters who had just come down from the fighting on Musa Dagh and got themselves cleaned up. Mourad brought along a box of Armenian pastry their mother had baked—baklava, sticky with nuts and honey.

Vinnie, Dik, and the three brothers sat in the recep-

tion room sipping espresso and eating pastry until Roy
Ashton appeared with his attaché case. He gave them a
startled look and turned them down when they invited
him to join them in their brunch.

"Who are all these people?" he asked Vinnie, laying
his attaché case on the table.

"Brothers of Dikran Arshagouni, here. He's about to
become my partner. Aram, Krikor, and Mourad—meet
Roy Ashton of Triskelion Enterprises. Roy Ashton—
Aram, Krikor, and Mourad Arshagouni."

"Pleased to meet you, *Baron* Ashton," said the
brothers evenly. *"Pari luiz."*

"Partner?" said Ashton, raising his white eyebrows.
"Have you signed any papers yet?"

"Not yet," said Vinnie.

"You'd be well advised not to."

"What does that mean?"

"I'm here to repeat the same offer I made to your
uncle on behalf of Triskelion, with a few added inducements."

Ashton then outlined the inducements, one of which
was a handsome salary for Vinnie, who was to be kept on
as manager of the winery for a minimum of eighteen
months. Vinnie didn't understand the other inducements
and said nothing. Dik did understand them, but didn't
say anything either. Ashton proceeded briskly, perhaps
under the impression that silence gives consent.

"You'd be wise to take us up on this offer—now—
before you mess it up with legal entanglements."

Vinnie looked at him owlishly through his black
horn-rims. "You put it more strongly than that on the
phone. You said 'if I knew what was good for me.' That
sounded kind of ominous."

"Take it any way you like."

"What if I gave you the same answer my uncle did?
Correction—I'm *giving* you the same answer my uncle
did: No. So is it still ominous?"

"If the shoe fits, wear it."

"Hey, that was well put," said Krikor. "Don't you think it was well put, Aram?"

"Sure. Sounds like Saroyan."

"I disagree," said Mourad.

"You *do!*" said Krikor. "How come?"

"He reminds me of a proverb our grandfather Khosrove used to repeat: 'One day they praised the ass's voice, and ever since he has brayed.' "

Ashton was irritated. "What is this? May I ask why these people are here?"

"They're sort of a council of advisors," said Vinnie.

"Then let *me* give you some advice straight out, Mr. Letessier. Number one, the people I represent have complete information concerning the financial predicament you're in, and number two, we *are* going to acquire this property—one way or another. You'd better understand that."

"You're sounding ominous again."

"Just as well. You apparently have no inkling of the powerful interests I represent, or how determined they are in this matter. They're an irresistible force and you, sir, qualify as a movable object. Perhaps I should say a removable object."

Dik spoke up. "Maybe Vinnie doesn't have an inkling, but we do. You don't need to waggle your eyebrows and hint around. We know all about Triskelion."

"All the better. But who exactly is 'we'?"

"My brothers and I belong to an organization called ARARAT."

"Never heard of it."

"The acronym stands for Armenians Reunited Against Racist Atrocities by Turks. And we know all about you too. You're a Turk."

"A *Turk?*"

"You can drop the pretense. We know your real name is Turgut Oyleet."

117

Ashton compressed his lips and glared at all of them. "I don't know what kind of stupid game you people are playing, but I don't find it humorous. In any case, for your information, no, I am not a Turk—not with a name like Ashton, and not with blond hair and gray eyes. Furthermore, Turk or not, my business here is with Vincent Letessier, so I respectfully ask all of you to butt out."

"We can't," said Mourad. "Temporarily, we're his bodyguard."

"Bodyguard?"

"Right. As you know, there have been some acts of violence around here—and what appear to be threats of violence. So we have a message for you: If anybody at all, at any time, carries out any kind of assault on Vinnie or Dikran, ARARAT will hold you personally responsible."

"This is crazy. Do you seriously mean to imply that Triskelion Enterprises had anything to do with Francis Letessier's murder?"

"It's possible. Sicily's emblem is a triskelion. Of course, you're not Sicilian yourself."

"No, I'm a Turk, right?"

"Right."

"Well, we *Turks* can't be blamed for the actions of every thug in the Napa Valley, can we? Nor can Triskelion, which is a legitimate business enterprise."

Aram spoke up. "What do you say we knock off the wrangling and just cut the Gordian knot? Mr. Ashton—or I should say Mr. Oyleet—we Armenians like to keep things blunt and simple, know what I mean? Make things clear. So here's the nut: If anything happens to Vinnie or Dik, we won't protest to either the police *or* Triskelion—we'll kill *you*. The world can do with one less Turk in it."

Ashton ran a hand over his hair and turned red-faced, which struck Vinnie as a distinct change for the better.

"I can't believe this! You're threatening *me?*"

118

"Why, yes. You'd be well advised to remember another of Grandfather Khosrove's old Armenian proverbs: 'The cat causes bad dreams to the mouse.' "

Ashton, still red-faced, gathered up his papers and rammed them into his attaché case. Turning to Vinnie, he said, "Is this your idea of how to conduct a business, Letessier?"

"Well, no," said Vinnie, "but these guys are Armenians and I can't do a thing with them. You know how they are. Proud. Vindictive. Touchy on the subject of genocide."

Ashton rolled his eyes and made for the door. As he went out he turned and said, "You'll be hearing from me."

As the sound of Ashton's departing stretch limo died away, Dik and his brothers roared with laughter. "I don't think we'll be hearing from him," said Mourad.

"I don't either," said Vinnie. "I'm glad to have *that* threat out of the way, but I'm no closer to finding out who killed Uncle Francis—or who put that dead body in the fermentation tank."

"You don't believe Triskelion had anything to do with it?"

"Oh, I think they had *something* to do with it. Look at this threat from Ashton, and the letter I saw that somebody at Triskelion sent to Nilla Toscana at the bank. The body in the tank—maybe. But I think murder would have been their last resort, not their first or second. My hunch is that somebody in the Valley is working with them, or at least is pulling stuff that works in their interest, and I intend to find out who."

"So what are you going to do next?"

"I think it's time I visited my ex-aunt Adrienne."

"Watch yourself with that one," said Dik with a grin. "Khosrove also used to say, 'There is no end to the wolf's appetite.' "

SEVENTEEN

Vinnie no longer traveled Zinfandel Lane unless he had to. He could not bear to see its junction with the St. Helena Highway, where Uncle Francis had died so ghastly a death. Instead he drove northwest on the Silverado Trail and turned left over the stone bridge onto Pope Street. He also tried not to look at the police station when he passed it.

Adrienne Letessier lived in a rented Spanish-style house with a red tile roof on Madrona Street, near Fir Hill Drive on the western edge of St. Helena. Two olive trees grew on the front lawn, but aside from two pots of thorny barrel cactus flanking the front door, that was it for vegetation—a low-maintenance house with a high-maintenance tenant.

Adrienne had sounded lukewarm at best when Vinnie phoned her, but agreed to let him stop by—for the sake of appearances, he sensed. She would have looked bad if she had said no.

Vinnie rang the bell. After a strategic pause, Adrienne opened the door. She was wearing white shorts again and a low-cut white cotton blouse with a bow at each bare shoulder. The cocktail glass in her left hand contained a pinkish drink that Vinnie, although his knowledge of mixology was rusty, thought might be either a virgin mary or an angel's tit—probably the latter, although either one would have meant she was indulging in Remembrance of Things Past.

"Hello," she said, looking him up and down as if she had never seen him before. "Come on in."

To Vinnie's surprise, Bert Craven appeared behind her.

"Hi, Vinnie," he said. "I've been giving Adrienne some tax and investment advice and I was just leaving. Adrienne, mind if talk to him a minute?"

"Be my guest. I'll leave the door open, Vinnie."

Bert stepped out into the entryway between the barrel cacti.

"Uh, Vinnie—have you signed any papers yet with Arshagouni?"

"You already know about that?"

"The word gets around."

"No, I haven't. Not yet."

"Don't."

"Oh?"

"Knowing you, Vinnie, I would guess you're about to give away the store."

"I like the deal. I'll still be co-owner."

"But with what percentage? And under what arrangement? Do you even know the legal difference between a partnership and a corporation? Do you *plan* to incorporate? You don't know? I didn't think so. Look—while you still can, take up Triskelion on their offer."

"Did you know they *threatened* me?"

"Threaten, shmeaten, their offer is still terrific. You'll come out of it rich. Put most of it into a mutual fund and live it up, and you'll never have to know a thing about finance or wineries or business management. I just recommended Massachusetts Growth Stock to Adrienne, and it'd be great for you too."

"Nope, won't do it. I love the Napa Valley and I love the winery and Dik Arshagouni is one hell of a guy."

Bert lifted both arms and slapped his thighs. "Okay, but at the very least let me go over the papers and make sure you aren't taken to the cleaners."

"Sorry, Bert. Hate to trash a deal for you, but no way."

"All *right*. Your *funeral*." He sauntered off down the walk. Because Bert was carrying neither a briefcase nor manila folders, Vinnie the Sleuth wondered if his connection with Adrienne entailed more than taxes and investments.

Entering the house, he passed through the entry hall and under an arch into the living room, his heels clicking on the Spanish tile floor. The room was furnished with massive, dark brown, indestructible-looking Mission-style breakfronts, a refectory table decorated with a serape runner and a Mexican vase full of huge paper poppies, and a thick plate-glass coffee table on which were nothing but a copy of *Wine Country* ("The Magazine From California's Wineland"), an ashtray full of cigarette butts, half of them lipstick-tipped, and a highball glass, behind which sat George Preston on a high, straight-backed Mission chair. He looked uncomfortable. The chair was so studded with knobs and bosses as to guarantee the sitter either lumbago or herniated nucleus pulposus—all very well for a monk bent on mortifying the flesh, but torture for a renter or the *chouchou* of a renter. Preston seemed willing to put up with anything, however, with whiskey as an analgesic, although Vinnie wondered if he, like Uncle Francis, was prepared to shell out twenty-five thousand dollars for each toss in the hay with Queen Adrienne.

Adrienne sat on a drum-shaped hassock, holding her cocktail in one hand and a cigarette in the other. "I believe you know George Preston."

"Long since. Hi, George."

" 'Lo."

"Care for a drink?"

She didn't seem to care much whether he did or not. "Sure—whatever you're having."

It proved to be quite a good strawberry daiquiri, not the erotic concoctions he had imagined.

"I hope this is a short social call," she said, "not a grilling. I've already been grilled by that woman detective. Holly Shelton. Where was I on the night of September whatever, and all that crap." She crossed her tan legs.

"No, no. Just filling in background about Uncle Francis. Who knows what might come up?"

"To make it short and sweet, neither George nor I killed your uncle, and we have no idea who did—or *did* you do it, sweetie pie?" she said to George, who looked at her glumly. "I certainly didn't do it. And you know why? Because I don't *need* anything. I've *got* everything I wanted." She darted an ash in the general direction of the ashtray. It lit on the magazine. She folded the magazine into a scoop, and dumped the ash into the ashtray. "Be pretty silly to screw myself out of five thousand a month, now wouldn't it? Somebody did, of course."

She took a drag on her cigarette, and blew the smoke out of both nostrils. Vinnie thought of a bull in the Tijuana bullring, pawing the sand and eyeing the torero's muleta.

"But I suppose you want to know—just in case—if

there was any 'ill feeling' between Francis and me. And the answer is, you bet your sweet ass there was."

"I sort of had a hunch there might be."

"When I married him I didn't know what I was getting into."

"He did."

Adrienne missed that one.

"He was a lousy husband and a lousy lover, Frenchman or not. And he had some weird habits. Like, he ate his toenails."

"Beg your pardon?"

"He'd lie in bed and pick at the corners of his toenails with a little bitty Swiss Army knife he had. He especially liked to dig out 'ingrowners,' he called them, and he'd put them on the end table by the bed, and later he'd chew them up and eat them."

"Well, you know the French," said Vinnie. "They can make a gourmet dish out of anything."

He thought that was a good one, but the other two didn't crack a smile.

Preston took a sip of his highball and fumbled a pack of Pall Malls out of his shirt pocket, lit one, and scowled through the smoke as he waved the match out.

"He was a horse's ass," he said. "When Adrienne broke up with him he took it out on me—and lost the best goddamn resident manager in the Valley, *if* you don't mind my saying so. Ask anybody. Even ask Gil Fernandez."

"He said you were pretty good. But after all, you *did* hook up with Adrienne."

"What difference did that make? After they broke up he didn't care, and Adrienne was free to 'hook up' with anybody she wanted to. Okay, so it happened to be me—but what did that have to do with my job?"

Vinnie thought the guy must be a real nerd if he didn't know, but evaded the question. "That's the breaks, I guess. So what are you doing these days?"

125

"Waiting for opportunity to knock. There's over two hundred wineries in Napa these days. Sooner or later somebody will need a good resident manager."

"You could always take your old job back while you're waiting, George," said Adrienne. "Bob Simmons said you could come back any time."

There was a trace of acid in the tone of her voice. Vinnie suspected that maybe Adrienne was getting a trifle impatient at having a freeloading boarder on her hands—one sitting around the house all the time—and that the two of them had talked about it. If so, Preston's position was shaky, because he was right: A footloose man-eater like Adrienne would have no trouble hooking up with somebody else, but in that case maybe he could try again with Nilla Toscana. Of course, if George was contributing his half of the expenses . . . or if the man was hung like a horse. . . .

"What job is that?" Vinnie asked.

"Oh, I used to be foreman of Bob Simmons's ranch up in the Alexander Valley. But hell, I'm an expert on winery operations now, and I don't want to take a step backward. Come to think of it, though, they've got wineries in the Alexander Valley." Suddenly, Preston gave Vinnie a species of smile. "Or how about you, Vincent? Keep in mind I know Château Letessier backward and forward."

"I've already given the job to Gil Fernandez."

"That son of a bitch. Well, lots of luck."

"What else do you need to know?" said Adrienne.

"I dunno. How about you? Do you plan to stick around in the Napa Valley?"

"Maybe. I like it here. But who knows?"

"Think you'll marry again?"

"Probably—if I find a guy that can make up for that five thou a month I've been aced out of." Preston picked up his highball and peered at her over the rim as he sipped. He didn't seem sure he was the people's choice at the moment.

"But what do you care?" she asked.

"I don't, really. Just beating my gums. Making conversation. Let me ask you, though: You lived with Uncle Francis at the winery for quite a while. Who would you say was most likely to want him . . . out of the way?"

She looked at him with a half smile and took a drag on her cigarette.

"You."

"*Me!*"

"Sure. He left you the winery, didn't he? And as I understand it, you didn't have a pot to piss in. Wasn't it 'lucky' you were his only relative."

"There was Delphine."

"Ha! Fat chance."

"Did you know who his enemies were?"

"Aside from George and me, if you want to call us that, sure: Those two guys he fired that drained his tank of cab. Andy Lacroix on the Board. I never trusted Bert Craven—married to Delphine; who knows what he was hoping? There's that uptight bigshot from Triskelion who bugged him all the time—probably Mafia, and half the members of the Vintners Association thought he was an asshole. Does that answer your question?"

"Maybe. By the way, where *did* you tell Holly Shelton you were the night Uncle Francis was killed?"

She smirked. "Just making conversation, were you? Well, Dick Tracy, I was visiting my parents overnight in Vallejo, okay? George drove me there."

"Did *he* stay overnight?"

"Ha! With those Southern Baptist parents of mine? Fat chance."

"So you drove back here, George?"

"Yes, and crawled into bed with my teddy bear, so knock off this shit."

"By the way, George, who had keys to the winery—especially the fermentation room?"

"Are you still whipping that dead horse of a practical joke? Keys? I did at one time, naturally. So did you. So did Francis and Gil Fernandez. So did Mrs. Barton for all I know."

"They hung on a goddamn nail," said Adrienne. "Anybody with a hunk of clay or a slice of bread or whatever could have taken an impression."

"Okay. Just asking."

"If that's all—nice of you to drop by," said Adrienne, smirking again.

Vinnie departed, not feeling he had learned much. Except that Bert Craven had some sort of relationship with Adrienne. Except that Preston could easily have gotten back to St. Helena the night Uncle Francis was killed, but so could everybody else. Except that his uncle ate his toenails. Some detective.

EIGHTEEN

Dikran Arshagouni was talking with Vinnie on the patio early one morning when Gil Fernandez emerged from the vineyard and hurried up to them, smiling, his white teeth gleaming in his tan face. He held a refractometer in his hand and seemed excited.

"Hey, you guys, want to see something interesting? Come with me."

"Where to?" said Vinnie.

"The eight acres of gewürztraminer up at the north end."

They were following him down the path toward the vineyard when a sheriff's department car pulled over onto the shoulder of the Silverado Trail, and Holly Shelton got out. She started up the slope toward them through the grass and flowers.

"Oh, oh, the fuzz is here," said Gil. "Ah, but what fuzz!"

Dik watched her as she approached, her honey-brown hair framing her face, shining in the sun.

"That kid doesn't know it yet," Gil said, "but she's going to marry me."

"I wouldn't count on it. She's always sounded pretty hostile."

"That's a good sign, man! Means she's involved with me."

"All right," said Vinnie. "But keep in mind your own Mexican proverb: '*Mira lo que haces antes que te cases.'* "

"Meaning what?" asked Dik.

"Look what you're doing *before* you get married."

"I thought you only knew French."

"I had to study Romance languages too."

Holly came up and joined the group. "Vinnie, I have a few things to tell you. Hello, Gil."

Fernandez raised his hands and grinned at her. "Not only was it self-defense, I wasn't even there," he said. "But arrest me anyway."

"Stop being silly."

Vinnie introduced her to Dik, who invited her to come along with them and see whatever it was Gil was excited about. Holly glanced at Gil.

"Sure, come on, Inspector," he said. "You'll be interested."

She followed the group, but hung back to talk to Vinnie.

"I found several human hairs and some rust-colored carpet fibers on Mifflin's shirt. The lab ran chromosome-staining procedures on the hair, and determined that it was a man's head-hair—but not Mifflin's. We don't know whose, of course. They also tried ABO typing, but didn't learn much of anything."

"What's that?"

"Trying to identify blood type from the hair. It looks as if—maybe—the blood type is O-negative, same as Mifflin's, but they aren't even sure of that."

"But if you found some guy with the same hair and same blood type, you'd have him nailed, wouldn't you?"

"Nope. It'd be indicative, and that's all. Some detectives think hair is as individual as fingerprints, but they're wrong. Of course, if we can connect a suspect with the hair and the blood type *and* the carpet fibers, we might have something."

"What kind of carpet is it? From somebody's house?"

"Maybe. But they're so short we think they're probably from a car, or maybe the ambulance 'Peter O'Toole' hauled Mifflin's body in."

"Sounds like a promising lead."

"Suuure—all we have to do is look at every car in the Napa Valley with rust-colored carpeting and give all the men a blood test. Anyway, I'm still putting heavy pressure on that dork Shira in Vacaville, trying to get a better description of the car and the driver, but he's scared shitless over getting nailed as an accomplice and losing his job. The prison authorities are grilling him too, and the medical school in San Francisco is raising holy hell with the prison. The dumb bastard is caught in the middle, so he's playing the injured innocent."

The discussion gave Vinnie an idea for a ploy he might be able to try on Lester Shira sometime, but it was so tentative he kept it to himself for the time being.

Meanwhile, marching along between the rows of vines, they arrived at the gewürztraminer acreage.

"Take a look at these grapes," said Gil. "You were right, Dikran. *Botrytis cinerea* everywhere—noble rot. Know what that is, Holly?"

"Who doesn't in Napa? A benign fungus. It sucks water out of the grapes and leaves a high concentration of sugar inside."

"Close, but no cigar. It doesn't suck, it just loosens the skin so water can evaporate, and we've been lucking out with these warm sunny days."

"What's the sugar reading at this point?" asked Dik.

"That's what I'm excited about. I've looked at grapes all over the vineyard with the refractometer, and the Brix reading is already thirty-three percent. If this dry weather holds, I'll bet it hits at least forty, maybe more. Anyway, it's up to you and Vinnie when you want to pick."

Dik turned to Vinnie. "What do you say—want to gamble?"

"In what way?"

"We could harvest in a week or so and make a first-rate dessert wine. Or, we could chance it and let the grapes stay on the vine until they shrivel and maybe—just maybe, unless some disaster hits—turn out an equivalent of the German *trockenbeerenauslese*."

"Translation for us peasants?" said Holly.

"Selected late-harvest dry grapes," said Vinnie.

"A dozen years ago," said Dik, "Joseph Phelps Vineyard did it with Johannisberg Riesling, and Blumberg gave it a twenty/twenty rating in *Wine Spectator*. 'Absolute perfection,' he said. 'Flawless, a treasure to own.' If we pulled this off, we could sell the stuff for forty or fifty bucks a half-bottle."

"Hell, let's give it a shot," said Vinnie. "What've we got to lose?"

"I agree," said Gil. "And *then* let 'em talk about 'body.' "

"Right," said Vinnie. "And speaking of body, I know what we could call this wine: Corpus Christi."

"Beautiful!" said Dik. "And we could release it on Corpus Christi day, with lots of advance publicity. Send a couple of bottles to Blumberg and Balzer."

"That's it, then, but let's hold our breath," said Gil, "and hope we aren't counting our Brix before it's batched."

On the way back through the vineyard, Vinnie told Holly about his talk with Adrienne Letessier and George Preston, but left out the most interesting item, the one concerning Francis's toenails. Holly was not much impressed but gave him a *C+* for effort; at least he had shed some light on Adrienne's possible motivation—and probable innocence—and Preston's shaky position as Adrienne's *chouchou* pro tem. "If Adrienne dumps him," she said, "he probably will have to take his old job at that ranch, which is too bad because he knows grapes and he really is a good resident manager."

"Not as good as Gil, I'll bet," said Vinnie. "Gil seems to know everything, and he's a lot nicer guy than Preston, don't you think?"

"He'll do—but don't tell him I said so. He's egotistical enough as it is."

Holly returned to her car, and Vinnie suggested to Dik that he and Satenig—Sandy—move in with him until they settled in a place of their own; or if they all got along well, maybe permanently.

"All right, thanks, we'll do it," said Dik. "However," he added with a laugh, "wouldn't that interfere with your love life?"

"I don't have one yet. Just working on it. How did you and Sandy meet, by the way?"

"At an Armenian picnic. It was more than her looks, it was her voice. My heart absolutely turned cartwheels when she got up and sang 'Groonk.' "

"Drunk?"

"No, dummy—'Groonk.' A groonk is a crane. It's a haunting Armenian song about a lonely crane soaring over the fields and mountains."

"Teach it to me. I'll sing it to Peggy."

NINETEEN

A s the warm days moved into October, noble rot puckered the grapes on the vines—and an airmail letter arrived in Vinnie's box from the Musée Jean Moulin in Bordeaux. Mostly because of his mild excitement, but partly because the lenses of his black horn-rims had butter smudges on them from his breakfast croissant, he delayed reading the letter until he could wash the lenses with soap and water in the bathroom. Then he sat down at the breakfast table and slit open the envelope with Uncle Francis's red-handled Swiss Army knife:

Monsieur Letessier—Several of my colleagues and I have read your letter and examined the enclosed photographs with live interest. Because of the passage of time since World War II, we cannot be certain of the identity of the man in the photographs, but his name—ANDRÉ GHISLAIN LACROIX—is identical to that of a Resistance fighter who died at the hands of the Gestapo in Limoges in February 1945. The man in the photographs is assuredly not the same person, of course, but the similarity of the names renders us highly suspicious. It appears at least possible that your Monsieur Lacroix entered the USA and became a citizen with spurious papers.

One of my colleagues, however, formerly a native of the city of Sarlat in the Department of Dordogne, informs me that the man in your photographs bears a passable resemblance to a certain JEAN-LUC PUTET, who betrayed to the Gestapo a Resistance network centered in Sarlat. A monument in the rue de la République of that city records that the members of that *réseau* were sent to Nazi extermination camps, where they suffered an atrocious death. Two surviving veterans of that *réseau* are more than eager to know if your Monsieur Lacroix is indeed this Jean-Luc Putet. If he is, they favor taking appropriate action to 'rectify the situation.' As you may know, the process of *épuration* has been going on ever since the war—finding and punishing the worst of collaborators according to French law. We have urged the veterans I mention to leave this matter to the authorities and subdue their expressed intention to personally "get their hands on" Putet.

Putet acquired the nickname *"la Sauterelle"*—"Grasshopper" in English—at that epoch, owing to his adroitness in jumping back and forth between the Germans and the Resistance. The Germans arrested him several times, but supposedly he always managed either to escape or talk his way out of detention. His "adroitness" was finally exposed as mere collaboration and ultimate betrayal.

However, before we or you make any hasty

accusations, we present a simple test for you to perform. Merely show your Monsieur Lacroix the enclosed card and observe how he reacts. It is an understatement to say that we shall be interested in the results. Awaiting your reply,

Agréez, Monsieur, l'expression de mes sentiments les plus distingués,

MARCEL FITE
Directeur

A calling card was enclosed, on which appeared a sketch and two words:

SARLAT —PUTET

Vinnie examined the card with curiosity and contemplated his next move. He decided against his original impulse—to show a photograph of Lacroix to Lester Shira at Vacaville—so as to prevent Shira from forewarning Lacroix. Instead, he drove into Napa once more and went up to Lacroix's office.

Lacroix again acted the part of the beaming host. "Come in! Sit down! Take a load off your feet! Glad to see you again. What can I do you for?"

The man's brown eyes focused alertly on Vinnie, his geniality obviously a mask for his mild puzzlement over the reason for this second visit.

"Some people in Bordeaux wanted me to show you something."

A stiff smile appeared on Lacroix's face. *"Bordeaux?* Who in Bordeaux?"

"The Musée Jean Moulin. It's a museum of the Resistance. Moulin was an organizer of the Resistance, sent by de Gaulle. The Gestapo tortured him and he died."

137

"I *know* that. Who would know better? What is this 'something' you're supposed to show me?"

Vinnie handed him the card. Lacroix took it without removing his glance from Vinnie's face.

Lacroix turned his back and went over to the window, presumably because the light was better there. He gazed at the card for a long while. When he turned about again, Vinnie was startled to see tears on the man's brown cheeks.

Lacroix could not meet Vinnie's eyes; he lowered his chin and his lips trembled. At last he took a deep breath and looked up. *"I was only eighteen!"*

Vinnie waited, numbed, silent. He had expected contemptuous laughter—scoffing—denial. Instead, Lacroix's—or Putet's—reaction was more that of a fugitive who knew he would be caught up sooner or later. The man's shoulders sagged.

"Barely eighteen! You have no idea what the Gestapo was like! What they did to me!"

"These people say you were just a collaborator."

Lacroix brushed the accusation aside, but Vinnie was sure the avengers in Sarlat had the goods on him.

Lacroix held up the card. He looked fear-stricken. "Do you—plan to—tell anyone about this?"

"The people in Bordeaux, I suppose."

"Don't do that, I beg of you! I was only a boy—a boy! Eighteen! They tortured me! I've begun a new life here! I've made up for things, surely you see that! Look at what I've accomplished—I'm a county supervisor! That was forty-five years ago! Please—forget the past, *je vous en supplie!"*

Taken aback by the man's emotional storm, Vinnie realized that he had not really thought through what he hoped to achieve, let alone the alternatives. What *was* his purpose? A little vague, wasn't it? Originally, his coming to see Lacroix had been little more than a shot in the dark, hoping to pick up some clues pointing to a conspiracy.

But this . . . Vinnie frowned and scratched the back of his head.

Seeing Vinnie's hesitancy, Lacroix made an effort to collect himself. "Can we make a deal?"

"What kind of a deal?"

"What if—what if I told you who put that body in your fermentation tank?"

Vinnie felt a surge of excitement.

"Vengeance," said Lacroix. "Revenge. After forty-five years. What would that mean to *you*? Nothing at all! But look what I am offering you! In exchange, all I ask— would you promise to forget this—this card?"

Vinnie made a snap decision. "Yes. I think I would."

"You really mean that?"

"Yes, I promise."

Lacroix's relief was immense. He hugged Vinnie and clapped both his shoulders. "I thank you. *Mille fois.* I thank you!"

"Who did?" asked Vinnie.

Lacroix swallowed and clenched his fists at his sides. *"I* did."

"May I ask why?"

"I did it for Nilla Toscana. She wanted Château Letessier ruined—and I wanted *her*, fool that I was. I used her station wagon. I kept the body hidden under party balloons until that night."

"So she knew all about it."

"Of course."

"But why? What was she going to get out of it?"

"Money. Triskelion Enterprises gave her fifty thousand dollars for her help, and she'd get another fifty if they ended up owning the winery."

"So. And how did you get into the fermentation room that night?"

"Picked the lock. We learned many useful tricks in

the Resistance," he said, with a rueful smile. "So—are we even?"

"Not hardly. There were thirty-nine hundred gallons of cabernet in that tank, worth a hundred and fifty thousand dollars. Write me a check."

Lacroix's tan paled a shade or two. "That would clean me out! It would take everything!"

"Pity." Vinnie shrugged. "But take your choice."

Lacroix, tight-lipped, got out his checkbook and pen.

"Make it out to the winery, not to me," said Vinnie.

Lacroix handed him the check.

"Oh—about that hotel . . ." Vinnie added.

"There will be no hotels."

"Triskelion is out?"

"Out."

"One last thing. Don't call Nilla. I want to surprise her."

"I won't." Lacroix heaved a bitter sigh. "So: Am I an American again?"

"True blue. Well, I'm off to the bank. I hope the check doesn't bounce."

"It won't."

TWENTY

Vinnie sat on a park bench under an olive tree in the Civic Center to reflect on his interview with Lacroix. A platoon of pigeons goose-stepped around him, hoping for bread or popcorn. He noted that most of them had made corporal, to judge by the chevrons on their wings. They broke ranks when they saw they were going to come up empty-clawed.

He had some misgivings about the interview. He was not at all sure he had done the right thing; but the situation was complex and he had instinctively zeroed in on what counted for his self-interest. He disliked Lacroix; the man was oily and devious and a liar, and probably deserved punishment for those long-ago sins in Sarlat, but perhaps his comeuppance, and the check in Vinnie's billfold, were punishment enough. He decided to talk the matter over with Peggy, who had cool good sense.

What impressed Vinnie most of all about the interview was . . . himself.

"The way I talked to the guy! That didn't sound like me at all! . . . *I was out of character!*" he marveled. "Maybe I'm getting some sort of noble rot myself. Without the sugar content."

Belatedly, anger rose within him over the truly filthy trick Lacroix and Nilla Toscana had attempted on Uncle Francis. What they had done was no prank, it was a felony, and by all rights they should both go to jail. And that raised another problem: Having accepted Lacroix's check and promised to keep his secret, Vinnie could not very well report the whole matter to Inspector Holly Shelton, now could he? No. But—disturbing thought—Holly being one hell of a sharp detective, she might solve the case anyway, and *then* what could he say or do? The TV screen in his mind flashed a picture of that female Sherlock Holmes with sparks of rage shooting out of her eyes. It made him squirm. She might even throw *him* in jail. He didn't know what laws he was breaking, but no doubt there was a handful.

It was too late to turn back now, however. "Oh, well—sheep as a lamb," he said to himself. He rose and strode toward the parking lot where he had left his Mercedes, contemplating with grim pleasure his forthcoming showdown with Nilla Toscana in St. Helena.

At the Vintners Bank, Nilla, unaware that she might well be a Millionaire in Detraining, sat at her desk talking on a telephone cradled between shoulder and chin, shuffling papers and scribbling an occasional note. Vinnie waited until she hung up before approaching her desk. She looked up at him with her Mediterranean blue eyes, but there was no warmth in them; it seemed to be off-season on the Amalfi Coast.

142

"And to what do I owe the honor this time, *Mr.* Letessier?"

"Your sins."

She looked puzzled, then amused.

"For which you're going to give me a lot of money," said Vinnie.

"If you're talking about another loan—"

"No, no. You're going to give it to me yourself. A hundred and fifty thousand."

"Have you been drinking?"

"I know all about the body in the tank, Nilla, and why it was in your station wagon hidden under balloons, and why you did it. So you're going to pay me damages."

Her nostrils dilated. "Do you realize I could sue you for slander? Would you mind repeating that in front of witnesses?"

"Sure. How about a VP or two? Call 'em over."

"I will! But would you mind telling me how you arrived at this craziness?"

"Oh, there's the evidence. Carpet fibers found on the body match the floor mats in your wagon, and there was a fragment of Mylar that came off one of the balloons." (Since the lab reports were due any time, he felt he wasn't really lying—just prevaricating).

She was incensed.

"So now you're a detective instead of an incompetent vintner. I think you'd better drop your nonsense and leave the case to Inspector Shelton."

"Incompetent, yes; nonsensical, no. I've been talking to Andy Lacroix."

She froze.

"As we detectives are fond of saying, the jig is up, *Miss* Toscana. Andy gave me a check for a hundred and fifty thousand, and more or less suggested I get the other half from you."

"*Other half!*"

"Yeah. His covers the loss of the tank of cabernet. Yours will cover punitive damages."

"You—this is extortion!"

"Right."

"You're the one that's a criminal!"

"Yeah. Fun, isn't it?"

"And what if I refuse to be extorted—which I can't be anyway?"

"You get fired and you go to jail. Still want some witnesses?"

She gave him a look of such ferocity that, had her tresses been snakes instead of glossy black hair, he would have turned to stone on the spot. Then the ferocity subsided into mere hatred. "You miss the point! I don't have a hundred and fifty thousand dollars. Where would I ever lay hands on that amount of money?"

"Up to you. You're a loan officer. Float yourself a loan. Or why not try Triskelion? You made a hell of a good effort, even if it didn't work out, so they should at least pay you the other fifty thousand they promised you. That'll help, won't it? Oh—if you write a check, make it out to the winery. I'll add it to our account and come back and catch up on our loan payments."

She glared at him.

"I'll give you exactly a week from today. Well, so long and good luck, Miss Toscana. I'll be waiting to hear from you."

Vinnie walked away, leaving Nilla in ruins like the Roman Forum.

TWENTY-ONE

Vinnie and Peggy dined on chicken marsala by candlelight at Château Letessier that evening. Both of them always refused to eat veal because of the inhumane way calves were treated, at least in California. So did Mrs. Barton, who prepared the meal. "We slaughtered 'em back in Missouri, but we didn't torture 'em," she said. She didn't much like that foreign idea, either, of pounding chicken breasts with a rubber mallet until they were a quarter of an inch thick, but had to admit it made cooking a lot easier, since they needed only two minutes or so on each side.

"This is truly delicious!" said Peggy. "What a cook she is!"

"She was good to start with, and Uncle Francis got

her into French cuisine. He could never get her to cook snails, though. She couldn't stand the sight of them—said she'd just as soon cook tumblebugs.''

"What are those?''

"Some kind of beetle back in Missouri that rolls dung into little balls and buries them and lays eggs in them.''

"*Bon appétit.*''

"Oh—sorry.''

"Too late . . . This sauvignon blanc is terrific, and I've already drunk too much of it.''

"So have I. We'll switch to a sauternes with the coconut cake.''

"Good idea.''

It being an unusually balmy evening—the warm, dry weather was holding—they took their cake plates and wineglasses out onto the flagstone patio, and sat side by side before a small wrought iron table. A bright gibbous moon shone on the round leaves of the silver-dollar eucalyptus trees. The shining leaves actually *looked* like silver dollars.

"*Le voilá que la lune distribue sa fortune.*''

"The moon does what?'' said Peggy.

"Distributes her fortune. Line of a song Jacqueline François used to sing. Pretty, isn't it? Is that another Orvis outfit you have on?''

"Yes,'' she said, slurring the *s* only faintly, "just got it today.''

She wore a red cotton calico blouse sprinkled with tiny flowers, and dark blue jeans. "I lucked out with the red moccasins,'' she said, extending two slim ankles. "I already had them. They match the blouse perfectly. The red belt came with the jeans.''

"It's a terrific-looking getup.''

"It's also warm, being brand new and sort of stiff. I may need your help.''

"Doing what?''

"Unbuttoning the blouse. The buttonholes are pretty tight."

He set his wineglass down on the table and gazed into her face. Her blue eyes, full of mischievous mirth, looked back at him beneath her black bangs.

"Oh, Peggy!"

Smiling, she rose and sat on his lap and put her arm around his shoulder. As they went into a long and fervent kiss, Vinnie fumbled at the top button with his right hand. And fumbled and fumbled. He would have had less trouble if women didn't button their clothes from left to right.

Peggy broke away, laughing. "Two hands for beginners." She leaned back, unbuttoned the blouse herself, and bared her small and round and lovely breasts to the blue-white light of the moon.

Vinnie kissed her nipples. Peggy trembled and leaned her head on his shoulder as he stroked her slender waist, and ran his fingers down the groove of her back.

Vinnie swallowed the tightness in his throat and murmured, "Uh, how are the jeans? Too warm? Too tight?"

"Both. I'll need even more help with those."

"Peggy, I love you."

"I love you, too, Hippomenes. I'm glad you threw those apples."

"I'm glad I went bankrupt so I could meet you," he said, kissing the upper slope of her right breast. "It's the best thing that ever happened to me. Everyone should try bankruptcy."

She bent and kissed him again, her black hair surrounding his face. Then they stood and walked back into the house together, arms around waists.

They went into Vinnie's bedroom on the ground floor. Vinnie opened the sliding glass door to the evening breeze that was ruffling the moonlit leaves of the vineyard just outside.

Two minutes later, naked, they stood in a close embrace, skin against skin, exhilarated by the freedom—the liberation—to be had by shedding clothing and banter and all pretense.

They moved to the bed, and Peggy held her arms out to him, smiling. He kissed her lips, cheeks, and neck, and went on to kiss the hollows of her shoulders and every other hollow and mound down the length of her firm, athletic body, including the ravines of her groin and her mound of Venus with its perfect small triangle of black hair, marveling all the way at her loveliness and the immense gift she was giving him. He finally entered her, completing the gift of himself, and she gasped in ecstasy.

Unfortunately, he gave too much too soon: At his eighth stroke, the overloaded, pent-up reservoir of his libido burst its barrier in an erotic analog of the Johnstown flood, the eruption of Mauna Kea, and—in this case misnamed—Old Faithful.

"Oh, God, Peggy! I'm sorry. It's . . . been too long."

She put her hands on his neck and kissed him. "It's all right. It's been far too long for me too."

He lay back with a sigh. "Maybe in ten or fifteen minutes."

"I can wait. Just being here like this is delightful."

"Okay, but this is hardly the way I imagined our first . . . get-together."

"Don't let it worry you. After all"—she gave him an impish smile—"the best-planned lays of mice and men gang aft agley."

"Oh! You—!" He snatched a hand towel from his end table and swung it at her leg. She sprang from the bed with a laugh, and ran outside onto the patio and into the vineyard, Vinnie two or three bed lengths behind. She fled away in the night between rows of cabernet vines, her body gleaming in the moonlight, her beauty amazing Vinnie still more. She was a marble Greek statue come to life; she was Galatea, Atalanta, Botticelli's Venus, but above all she was Peggy Singletary, the great love of his life.

He caught up with her, and she laughed and stumbled and fell as he flicked her peach-like bottom with the hand towel. She was the most beautiful thing Vinnie had ever seen in his life. He gazed at her as she lay on the ground bathed in moonlight, in this bower of grape leaves.

She was also the most erotic thing he had ever seen. He knelt before her and Peggy's knees parted. And this time, when they joined and moved together in their love, it lasted until the lower limb of the moon touched the western hills.

Later, after showering, they lay together on Vinnie's bed, her right leg over his left, wordless for a long interval, until Vinnie broke the silence.

"You're a real liberated woman, aren't you, Peggy?"

"Ha! The answer to that is what Lauren Bacall said to the Shah of Iran when told she was a good dancer: 'You bet your ass, Shah.' "

Vinnie laughed. "Wonderful. Okay, let me say this to you: Will you marry me, Peggy—and if so, will you promise to stay liberated?"

"The answer is yes to both questions."

They made love again and afterward, this time, Vinnie lay a long while in thoughtful silence.

"Feeling *tristesse?*" asked Peggy.

"Sort of, but only because of what happened today. It bothers me. Do you think I did the right thing with Lacroix?"

She thought it over, one hand under her head. "As opposed to just going away and notifying the people in France? I don't know. I'm not sure there is a right answer. Maybe you could get one from a philosopher or a theologian, but not a custom-tile designer."

"Well, what do you think *you* would have done in my place?"

149

"What you did. You had to make a quick choice between justice for something he did forty-five years ago and justice for something he did here. All right, you chose in your own self-interest, and he's been punished. So has Nilla Toscana."

"Yes, but he didn't cause anybody's death here in Napa."

"Oh? Has it occurred to you he might have been the one that killed your uncle? Maybe with another one of his Resistance tricks?"

"You're going to think I'm a silly ass, but no, it hasn't. Anyway, I don't think he did."

"Why not?"

"Just a feeling."

She touched his nose with a fingertip. *"That* is not very detective-like, Tweetie-pie."

"Yeah, you're right, of course. Back to the magnifying glass. Meanwhile, what do I tell those people in France?"

"I'm afraid you'll just have to lie to them. . . . Uh—speaking of lying, Sugar Plum, come April, how are you going to explain those big checks to the IRS?"

"Oh, oh."

They lay for half a minute or so in what Lewis Carroll would have called uffish thought, until Peggy spoke.

"Why don't you ask Bert Craven for ideas? He's so crooked he could hide behind a corkscrew."

"Good idea. I'll have to lie to him too, of course." Vinnie sighed. "Damn it, Peggy, I think I'm getting used to lying."

"Mark Twain had the right idea. He said you should never lie unless it's absolutely convenient."

TWENTY-TWO

B ert Craven lived on Stonehouse Drive in Napa.
Seating himself behind his desk, he exited the display on his Macintosh computer, switched it off,
moved a stack of papers to the top of his Hewlett-Packard
printer, and looked at Vinnie with alert and curious eyes.

"When did you come into this money?"

"I didn't say I had it, I'm just saying what if—a
hypothetical case."

"And you want to know how to launder it for the
IRS."

"If you want to call it that."

"What else are you going to call it?"

"I was kind of hoping for something . . . legal."

"Doesn't sound like it to *me*. Let's stick to laundry.

Okay: The best way I know of is go to Las *Vegas,* pick out a *football* game—make that *five* games—and bet X dollars on both teams in each game. You bet *both* sides. Got it? Obviously, you'll *win* five bets and you'll *lose* five bets."

"And declare the losses?"

"No. You can only declare losses against winnings. So—let's say you end up ahead of the game by Y dollars, so you have to pay maybe a net five-percent tax—which is not bad at *all,* considering you can now leave with clean *money.*"

"I'm not sure I understand all that. Anyway, the bets would have to be in cash, wouldn't they?"

"Well, sure."

"What if it's, oh, let's say a check."

"A big check? That's different. *Now,* you've got a *problem.* Forget Vegas."

Bert chewed on a pencil, frowning. Perhaps he had bitten into some bad cedar. Vinnie could almost see a Macintosh program called "Fox the Feds" lighting up on the screen of Bert's brain. Finally, Bert finished his mental scrolling and laid the pencil down.

"Here's a possibility. You say you won a bet, like which raindrop got to the bottom of the window first. Or better yet: You could say on your ten-forty it's for settlement of a dispute. How about that one? Would that work?"

Vinnie was delighted and relieved, but tried to keep it from showing. (Of course it would work! That's just what it was: settlement of a dispute. Two of 'em, to be exact.)

"I suppose it would. Mind you, all of this is . . . just in case."

"How much money are we talking about?"

"Oh, no particular amount. I just want to be thinking ahead, that's all."

"You'd better, if you want to stay out of jail."

Vinnie got out of his chair. "Well, thanks a lot for

152

the advice, Bert. I really appreciate it." He turned to go.

"Wait a minute. That'll be a hundred bucks."

"Oh! Sure."

Vinnie wrote a check as Bert looked him over—speculating . . . pondering.

TWENTY-THREE

I saw you coming out of the County Building yester-day," said Holly Shelton. "Who were you visiting?"

"Andy Lacroix."

"I thought so. Second time, wasn't it?"

Vinnie retreated a step and leaned against the window of Vasconi Drugs.

"Yeah, how did you know?"

"The word gets around. I suppose you were sleuth-ing; did you find out anything?"

"Nothing much. He's got the hots for Nilla Tos-cana."

"So do half the men—and a few women—from Napa to Calistoga. Anything else?"

Vinnie rubbed the back of his head and fingered an

eyebrow. "Oh, I guess you could call it good news. It looks as if he'll oppose any new hotels or motels or what-not in the Napa Valley."

"That *is* a surprise. He's always been pretty gung ho for development. He told you that, or was that just your impression?"

"He said it."

"And that's all you found out?"

"Yeah, I suppose that's it."

"So you two just had a chummy get-together. Apparently he likes you a hell of a lot better than he did your uncle."

"Guess so. One never knows."

Inspector Shelton's blue eyes looked straight through Vinnie's corneas, retinas, and brain, out the back of his head, through the show window, and on into the interior of Vasconi Drugs.

"Were you going to report this conversation to me?"

"Gee, I don't know. There was nothing much to report, really."

"Vincent, you're acting antsy. What are you holding back?"

He gave her an owlish look through his black horn-rims.

"Nothing. Not a thing."

"How come you went to see Lacroix a second time? Not over hotels, was it? I should think that Triskelion business was a dead issue, now that Arshagouni is buying into your winery."

"Oh, I knew he had a connection with Nilla Toscana, and Nilla seemed to want Château Letessier to fail and had some kind of connection with Triskelion, so I thought maybe I could pry something out of him that had . . . something to do . . . with the body in the tank. If you follow me."

"I follow you. But I think you'd be better off paying more attention to your winery, and less to sleuthing."

"Maybe so. I don't seem to be getting anywhere."

"Not that I'm doing much better. That nerd Shira over in Vacaville is so terrified of getting mixed up in a felony he's buttoned his lip to the tip of his nose."

"How about the murder?"

"I have some leads I'm working on. All right, I'll let you go. I think I'll call on Lacroix myself. And if you have any more conversations like that, you *will* report them to me, right?"

"Sure thing."

Holly strode off down Main Street, her honey-blond hair bouncing against her collar. When she turned into the Model Bakery and disappeared, the knot in Vinnie's stomach unwound a coil or two, but "what if she finds out the truth?" he asked himself. "Which she is quite likely to do. My god, my cook will be goosed!" He realized he had not thought through the consequences. As ignorant of the law as he was of money matters, he wondered if the law would have allowed him to drop charges against Lacroix. Would "society" give a damn if he dropped charges? After all, Lacroix's crime was mostly against the winery, not against the people of California— wasn't it? Or was this totally a police matter, out of his hands? Oh—but what about that body from Vacaville? "Society" might have a shit hemorrhage over that one. What a mess!

He passed the rest of the day in a state of anxiety and morosity. He was morose mainly because Peggy was in San Francisco, buying glazes and art supplies and visiting friends, and would not be back until late that night. She had already gotten a new comission from the Königsberg Winery.

"Karl-Heinz Königsberg was so impressed with the mural I did for Clos d'Ausone, now *he* wants a poem on tile—a German one that begins *'Uber allen Gipfeln ist Ruh'*. He says it's Goethe's most famous poem, and I have to do it in Gothic lettering."

Feeling at loose ends that evening, and not wanting to play hearts or dominoes or hop ching or whatever with Mrs. Barton, he fed Ezra a bowl of Science Diet, got in his Mercedes, and drove north of St. Helena on Highway 29 to the Cement Works, a shopping center comprising an assortment of stores and a cozy pub, the Hare and the Tortoise.

He eased onto a padded bar stool at the pub. An icy Crystal Stolichnaya on the rocks calmed him down and lifted his optimism a notch. He began to feel at peace with the world and more tolerant of mankind—even including the scruffy dude drinking nonalcoholic beer on the next stool but one.

The dude appeared to be twenty-four or twenty-five. His stringy blond hair brushed the collar of his faded blue-denim jacket. His neck was scrawny, fiery red, and pitted like the craters of the moon. That was okay with Vinnie. Takes all kinds. He reminded Vinnie of Tafardel, the schoolmaster in Chevallier's *Clochemerle,* who prided himself on his irresistible powers of persuasion, whereas in truth his breath was so ghastly that when he button-holed his fellow Beaujolais villagers, they would agree right away to anything he proposed, and then flee.

Suddenly, the man put his hands on the bar and turned to Vinnie with a piercing look. "Brother, how's your soul?" he said in a sepulchral voice.

Startled, Vinnie shrugged his shoulders and said, "Okay, last time I looked."

The man frowned at that reply. "A friendly warning: It says in Matthew that every idle word will be accounted for on Judgment Day."

"It does, does it? Then somebody is in for a really dull clerical job."

"You won't be so breezy when you find yourself in danger of hellfire."

"Oh well, in the meantime *ora pro nobis peccatoribus.*"

"You're a Catholic."

"Nope."

"How come the Latin then?"

"Academic requirement."

The man slid onto the stool next to Vinnie. "May I ask your name?"

"Sure."

Vinnie sipped his drink. The man stared at him. "Well?"

"Well what?"

"What's your name?"

"Pippick," said Vinnie. "Moshe Pippick."

"You don't look Jewish."

"Neither do you."

"I'm not."

"Neither am I," said Vinnie. "We're having trouble getting to the nut, aren't we?"

"As a Christian, I'm concerned about your immortal soul, and I'd like to help you get on the right path."

"How do you know I'm not already on it?"

"You don't talk like a Christian."

"Let's say I'm a Christian with a small *c*."

"I thought so. You don't have *faith*."

"Sure, but don't forget: *Fides sine operibus mortua est.*"

"Meaning what?"

"Faith without good works is dead. Which is why I'll buy you another one of those beers if you're ready."

"All right, I thank you."

Vinnie ordered another round. He was vaguely aware of what was going on in his head. He was unhappy and petulant because Peggy wasn't there, so he was acting it out by talking pure balderdash with this stranger.

"If you're not Jewish," said the man, "what is your background?"

"You might say I'm Nisei French."

"French, hey? So what's your real name?"

"Covaire," said Vinnie. "Harry Covaire."

159

"I suppose you're connected with one of those wineries."

"Nope. There's no liaison with Harry Covaire."

The French I lesson went over the man's head.

"I'm glad to hear it. This whole valley is one big sink of iniquity. I'd like to see all the wineries shut down and the Valley go back to farming. If they want to raise table grapes, fine, but why turn them into alcohol? 'Look not upon the wine when it is red, for it biteth like a serpent and stingeth like an adder.' Proverbs Twenty-three."

"You must be from that college in Angwin."

"Part-time student. By the way, my name's Bontrager—Leonard Bontrager."

He shook hands with Vinnie.

"And how's your own soul?" asked Vinnie. "Plugging along okay?"

"Oh, I'm a sinner like everyone else. I've done things I'm ashamed of. Rotten things, sometimes."

"Like taking potshots at winery trucks?"

"No, no. That was a mentally ill student who just went berserk. He was lucky he didn't kill anybody. I'd sure hate to have killing on my conscience! No, about the worst I ever did was play a dirty trick on somebody—for money. 'The love of money is the root of all evil.' First Timothy."

"What kind of dirty trick?"

"Putting sugar in a guy's gas tank to gum up the carburetor."

Vinnie's heart gave a thump. He scrutinized his drink, stirring the ice cubes with a forefinger to cover the alertness that must have shown on his face.

"You got money for this?"

"I pump gas down the road a piece. One night a fella came up and gave me twenty-five bucks if I'd drop this capsule full of sugar into the tank I was filling. The owner had gone to the rest room."

"What kind of car was it? Big one?"

"No, kind of small. Black, looked sort of foreign. Sounds dumb, but I hardly know one car from another. Cars never interested me. Anyway, I didn't want to do it but the fella said the driver had been making time with his wife and he wanted to teach him a lesson. Well, I figured, sure—an adulterer had what was coming to him, and I needed money, so I did it."

Although he was excited, Vinnie felt it wise to restrain himself and go slow with Bontrager. Not knowing the man, he had no idea how Bontrager might react to the possibility of being involved in a murder—if indeed that was Uncle Francis's car. This was definitely a case for Super Holly, not him.

"How long ago was that?" he asked as casually as he could.

"Three weeks or so. I sorely repented it later. If I knew who the guy was I'd give the money back to clear my conscience."

"You wouldn't recognize him if you saw him again?"

"Never saw him before and haven't seen him since. Probably wouldn't recognize him if I did. He was wearing a wool-knit cap down to his eyebrows and had a mustache that looked like a Hershey bar. Maybe I'd recognize the mustache."

"Local guy, do you think?"

"I wouldn't know. I live on Brannan Street up in Calistoga."

"Want me to drop you a line in case I run into him? That mustache sounds like an eye-catcher."

"I'd appreciate it, sure. That'd be right *Christian* of you, Harry," he said, with a roguish smile.

He wrote his address on a cocktail napkin and gave it to Vinnie.

"Well, I've got to be shoving," said Bontrager. "You give some thought to your soul, now!"

"I'll give the bugger a thorough going-over, Leonard. See you."

High excitement being a renowned stimulus for the bladder, Vinnie asked the bartender for directions and made his way through the tables to the men's rest room. The place was almost half full—not a bad crowd for a Wednesday evening.

In the rest room Vinnie had to restrain himself again, for a janitor was working on the lone urinal. The janitor was a tall, gawky man with no chin, a protuberant Adam's apple, and a tic that made his eyes squeeze shut every few seconds. Peering at the urinal as he manipulated a snake, he gave Vinnie a brief glance.

"Just be a minute," he said. "I do sorely wish the fellas wouldn't throw filter cigarette butts in here." He gave the snake a vigorous push and twist, and was rewarded with a noisy burbling followed by a loud hydraulic borborygmus.

The janitor was delighted. "There she goes!" he said to Vinnie. "When the old bubbles start coming up, you know she's clear!"

Vinnie remained speechless for a moment, fascinated to hear a urinal referred to as "she"; but he complimented the janitor on his victory as he gathered up his equipment and went out.

Standing at the urinal, Vinnie perused the various graffiti on the wall, the best of which informed him that "This is where Napoleon took his Bonaparte."

Behind him, he heard the door to one of the stalls being unlatched, but he followed male protocol by not looking around at the man who came out. Isn't done. He later wished he had looked, for an unseen hand suddenly slammed his forehead into the tile wall.

He came to fifteen or twenty minutes later, lying on the rest-room floor with Bert Craven kneeling beside him asking if he was "all right."

Vinnie was not all right. Bert called the medics, who

took Vinnie off to Queen of the Valley Hospital on Trancas Street in Napa. The doctor there insisted that he stay at least overnight for observation, even though he was ambulatory, because he had a brain concussion. That was obvious, since Vinnie had no recollection at all of what had happened—a fact that made the note he found in his shirt pocket all the more puzzling.

The note was printed in block letters on a fragment of newspaper. It read simply, "Just a warning—*this* time. We think you know what you have to do next. Like sell."

TWENTY-FOUR

Vinnie woke up in his hospital bed at nine the next morning with a headache, dizziness, and a pink knob on his forehead, common features of post-concussional syndrome, according to the young doctor who examined him. The doctor also asked him a series of questions that Vinnie, although he had trouble concentrating, found a hell of a lot easier than his M.A. oral at UCLA: What was his name, how old was he, what day of the week was it, what was the name of the place where the assault occurred, what's the capital of California. The only one he missed was the day of the week, but he had to struggle to remember the Hare and the Tortoise. All in all, 80 percent wasn't bad, but he was glad the doctor didn't want to know, for example, the capital of Missouri. Mrs. Barton would have been chagrined.

"I think you can get dressed and go home if somebody drives you," said the doctor. "Maybe one of your visitors."

The doctor left and two young women came into the room, one of whom Vinnie wanted to see—Peggy Singletary—and one that he didn't—Holly Shelton. Peggy hurried to the bed and gave him a hug and a kiss, and inundated him with words of sympathy and worry. Holly was sympathetic, but was there on business. Once Peggy had finished emoting and saying how worried she had been, Holly began with the questions.

"What's the last thing you remember doing?"

"Reading graffiti and peeing."

"And just before that?"

"A janitor was unplugging the urinal."

"Did he leave?"

"Yes. The urinal bubbled up and she was clear."

"She?" Holly was disgusted.

"That's what he called . . . her."

"So you were alone in the rest room?"

"Yes."

"Then who clobbered you? God?"

"I don't know."

"Well, *somebody* was in that rest room."

"Wait a minute! I remember now—I heard a door open to one of the stalls."

"Then that was your man. We have to assume it *was* a man."

Vinnie pondered.

"Hey, I just realized something else."

"What?"

"I didn't hear any flushing."

"Ah, ha! So someone was in the pub the same time you were, and bet you'd go to the men's room sooner or later. You were ambushed. . . . And when you came to, that Good Samaritan Bert Craven was bent over you and took care of everything. Wasn't that a happy coincidence? And who was *he* there with?"

"I don't know."

"Did you know anyone else in the Hare and the Tortoise?"

"Only a new acquaintance—sort of a religious eccentric named Leonard Bontrager. I've got his address in Calistoga."

"All right, I've got some interrogating to do."

"So do I, if you don't mind."

"Go ahead. I guess you're entitled."

Holly started for the door, but turned around. "One more thing, Vincent. This isn't an appropriate time to ask—or maybe it is—but do you have a will? No? Then may I suggest you draw one up right away, just in case?"

"Ah yes, I see your point."

"You realize in case you croaked intestate, your next of kin would inherit, and your next of kin is Delphine Craven. Who is married to your Good Samaritan."

"The plot thickens."

"Doesn't it, though?" Holly left.

Vinnie frowned, thoughtful.

"Peggy, maybe we'd better get married right away so you'll be my next of kin," said Vinnie.

"I'm all for it. But you take care of yourself, Vincent Letessier! If you get yourself murdered, darn it, I'll never forgive you!"

"Have no fear. Did you know that St. Vincent is the patron saint of vintners?"

"What does that have to do with anything?"

"And are you aware that you must be part French yourself?"

"Is your mind wandering, or are you just feeling better?"

"Both."

"I'm English-Scotch-Irish."

"The name Singletary is a corruption of St. Gaultier,

which is in France. Sort of like Bewley from Beaulieu or Beecham from Beauchamp."

"I'm taking you home and you are going to lie down for the rest of the day."

"I heard that!" Dikran Arshagouni came into the room. "Hey, you're going home? That's great news, partner!" After Vinnie brought him up to date on all that had happened, Dik laughed and said he had another piece of interesting news. "Turgut Oyleet, also known as Roy Ashton, put in a frantic call to the winery this morning and got hold of Gil Fernandez. His message was—and he said it about six times with lots of emphasis—he had absolutely nothing to do with this attack on you, and neither did anybody else at Triskelion. The guy was scared spitless."

"How did *he* hear about it so quick?"

"I called him after *I* heard about it from Peggy. He had his office and home phone numbers on the business cards he gave us, remember? I left a message on his answering machine."

"I agree with him. I don't think that was Turgut in the men's room."

"Vinnie—get dressed. Let's go home."

"Right. . . . Hey, Dik, who actually is Turgut Oyleet?"

Dik laughed. "He's a wild-looking mechanic in one of George Booth's *New Yorker* cartoons."

TWENTY-FIVE

Vinnie's head cleared up sufficiently by noon the next day for him to hit on a possible but very shaky solution to a serious problem. He sought out Gil Fernandez in the bottling room, where he was lunching on pizza and a glass of cabernet.

"I've got a favor to ask, Gil—a big, *big* favor."

"You name it, boss."

"First, I want you to phone Holly Shelton."

"Me? Phone *Holly?*"

"Ask her to come up here because we have something important to tell her."

"Why don't you phone?"

"Because I'm scared of her and you aren't."

"I have my moments. She threw me in jail, you know."

"She might throw *me* in jail when I tell you the rest of it."

"Which is?"

"Listen, Gil, I'm going to tell you some stuff that has got to remain strictly between you and me. Absolutely secret. Mum's the word. Signed in blood. Can I trust you?"

"Sure. I *like* my job. . . . Forget I said that, Vinnie. You can rely on me."

"Okay. I want you to persuade Holly to drop the case of that body in the tank."

"Uh huh."

"No, really, and I'll tell you why. I know who did it, and I've already made the two people involved pay double what it cost us. So I'm willing to call it even."

"Are you going to tell me who they were?"

"Andy Lacroix and Nilla Toscana."

"*Jesús, María, y San José!* Lacroix! A *supervisor?* How did you find out?"

"Oh, clues. I put two and two together and confronted Lacroix." Vinnie forbore mentioning Lacroix's peril at the hands of the Resistance. "So you see my problem. Sure, Holly could solve the case and make an arrest—and that would blow those two people out of the water, I'd have to return the money, and I'll bet she would nail me for obstruction of justice."

"And you want *me* to ask her to call off the dogs."

"I'll do it with you."

Fernandez grinned, white teeth brilliant in his tanned face.

"All right, let's give it a shot. I always wanted to see a volcanic eruption."

Holly showed up at 1:00, none too happy. "This had better be worth interrupting my lunch for."

"Mine was interrupted too," said Gil.

"So what's the story?"

Gil laid out the facts, naming names and making the request.

Holly turned to Vinnie. "Well, Sherlock. You turned out to be quite the hard-boiled PI."

"Oh—poached, maybe."

"Why aren't you telling me all this instead of Gil?"

"I thought because you two know each other better."

"*And,*" said Gil, "this isn't just for Vinnie, it's for the whole winery—including me."

"What do you have to do with it?"

"I'm resident manager—Super Mex, like Lee Trevino and Chi Chi Rodriguez."

"Rodriguez is Puerto Rican."

"Same thing. Anyway, I'm respectable now—just what you always wanted. And I want to hang on to this job."

"And you two want *me* to stop doing *my* job. You've got one hell of a nerve, I must say."

"Look at it this way, Inspector Shelton," said Vinnie. "I'm happy, I've been repaid, I don't hold any grudges, and I don't see any point in destroying two people after the fact. They've already been punished."

"Not in my book. Those two committed a felony. The answer is no."

Vinnie shoved his hands in his pockets and chewed his lip.

Holly glared at him. "You will also tell me, Mr. Letessier, exactly how you got on to Lacroix. Come on, let's have it."

Reluctantly, Vinnie saw he would have to turn up his hole card. He told Holly about Lacroix's betrayal of the French Resistance. "So you see, the guy's life is in danger. Really. Do you want to see him killed now, over what amounts to no more than a dirty trick?"

Holly hesitated, thinking it over.

"The important thing," Vinnie added, "is Uncle

Francis's murder. I certainly want you to do your job on that."

Holly considered for several long moments.

"All right, I'll go along—but let me tell *you* something important. I solved the case myself this morning. I was going to arrest Lacroix this afternoon and haul Nilla Toscana in for questioning tomorrow."

Vinnie was stunned. "How did you do that?"

"I hauled that numbnuts Lester Shira down to Napa this morning and took him through the jail, for starters. That shook him up. Then I grilled the bastard—showed him pictures of some of our male suspects and nonsuspects, and he finally fingered Lacroix."

"How about Nilla?"

"The Triskelion connection and Lacroix's infatuation with her. I got a search warrant and hit paydirt right off with her station wagon, which was unlocked. I collected some carpet fibers and human hairs—no Mylar balloons, though. All I need now are the lab results, and I know what they're going to be."

"I thought Lacroix used an ambulance."

"No doubt he did, but they transferred Mifflin's body to the station wagon. They couldn't very well sneak up to the winery in an ambulance."

"This knocks me out," said Gil. "Both of you solving the case—Vinnie by accident, and you by real detective work. *Estupendo,* Holly!"

"*No eches flores.*"

"Hey! I didn't know you speak Spanish!"

"Now you know."

"And I *wasn't* just flattering you. I think you're a hell of a gumshoe—and at long last it looks like you're going to give me a date."

"What makes you think so?"

"I caught the *tú* form of that verb, *Chiquita.*"

Holly gave him a small smile. "I'll think about it."

"Over dinner tonight."

172

"Dutch."

"You're on. Seven."

"Back to work," said Holly. "On with the murder case, and that assault on you, Vinnie. I'll start with the Hare and the Tortoise."

"You've given me an idea too," said Vinnie. "I'll go talk to Bontrager."

"All right, but watch yourself. And damn it, keep me informed! You aren't dealing with a prankster this time. The guy's a murderer."

Vinnie met Leonard Bontrager again sooner than he had planned, when he stopped for gas at the Texaco station in St. Helena. He had just inserted the unleaded-gas nozzle in his tank when Bontrager appeared at his side.

"Hello there!"

"Why, hello, Leonard! So this is where you work."

"Yep. Sure is a pretty red car you got there. What kind is it?"

"Mercedes."

"Here—let me get that windshield for you."

Bontrager took up a squeegee from a nearby bucket and went to work.

"How come you're doing that, Leonard? This is the self-service line."

"You might say I like to sow my seed on good ground because it'll be returned a hundredfold. Luke Eight." He carefully drew the squeegee across the glass. "Saw your picture in the paper with your name underneath—Vincent Letessier. How come you told me Harry Covaire?"

"Sorry. Just a private joke of mine."

"It also said you own a winery."

"Yeah, I do. I admit it. Will you still finish my windshield?"

Bontrager laughed. "Well, Jesus turned water into wine at the marriage feast, so it can't be all bad. . . . I was right sorry to read about somebody knocking you in the head.''

"Yeah, it came as a blow to me too.''

Bontrager grinned and put the squeegee back in the bucket. "You're quite a funny fella, you know that? Say, remember the man I told you about at the Hare and Tortoise? The one I played the dirty trick for? Darned if I didn't see him again that same night you got conked! Talk about your coincidences!''

"You *saw* him? Did you talk to him?''

"Tried to, but he was walking real fast out of the parking lot. At first I wasn't going to say anything at all because I was embarrassed. I didn't *have* the twenty-five dollars I wanted to give back to him, so it would have looked kind of silly—but then I thought I should at least get his name and address, so I ran after him.''

"Did you get it?''

"No. I tried to talk to him but he wouldn't stop—just waved me off and said 'forget it' and kept walking. Didn't even turn his head. So I thought fine, I'll just tithe two-fifty and let it go at that.''

"Listen, Leonard, I'm eager to get in touch with that guy myself.''

"How come? You didn't play a dirty trick for him too, did you?''

"No, I think he played a really bad one on me. I also think that Hershey bar mustache is a fake. Look—if I brought you a bunch of pictures of guys with mustaches and knit caps, think you could pick him out?''

Bontrager frowned. "Is he a criminal or something? I sure don't want to bear any false witness.''

"I'm not sure whether he is or not. But give it a try, okay?''

"Well, all right. I guess you still have my address in Calistoga?''

"Yes. I'll give you a ring when I'm ready.''

"Fine. That'll be twelve dollars even for the gas.''

Vinnie gave him the money, and slid behind the wheel of the Mercedes. "Leonard," he said, "if you see that guy again, stay away from him. He may be dangerous—and I don't think he liked your seeing him that night."

Vinnie drove away, leaving behind a puzzled Bontrager.

TWENTY-SIX

"This turned out to be interesting," said Holly, "Old Home Week at the Hare and the Tortoise. The bartender says practically the whole gang was in and out at one time or another. Bert Craven was there, of course, but guess who he was with—Nilla Toscana."

Vinnie's eyebrows rose. "You're sure it wasn't Delphine?"

"You're not up on things. Delphine got a job as cocktail waitress at the Auberge du Soleil and was working that evening."

"Who else was there? Andy Lacroix, I suppose."

"Nope."

"So I guess that lets him out."

"Not necessarily. The rest rooms at the Hare and the Tortoise are down a hall at the back, and there's a door at the end leading from outside. Anybody could have come in from the back and gone into the men's room, including Lacroix, Preston, Bert Craven, or a hired thug—who could even be your pal Leonard Bontrager taking on his second chore. I also asked the bartender if he saw anybody with a bushy mustache. He said no."

"At least that eliminates all the women," said Vinnie.

"Presumably."

"Although it *could* have been a woman—you know—in men's clothes."

"Let's not get dramatic."

"Guess you're right. So where do you go from here?"

"Get tighter information on these guys' movements. I'm especially interested in talking to Bontrager."

"Let me talk to him. You'll scare him if he finds out he's helped commit a murder. Look at what happened with Shira. Bontrager likes me, and I've got an idea what to do with him."

"Fine. I need to have another chat with Bert Craven anyway."

Vinnie went up to Peggy's house and found her busy doing a grid-paper layout of the Goethe poem. They exchanged hugs and passionate kisses.

"All right if I interrupt you, Peg?" said Vinnie.

"You just did. Nicely too."

"I need your artistic talents."

Vinnie handed her a sheaf of photos, four on photographic print paper, one from the *St. Helena Star,* in which the faces appeared of Vinnie without his black horn-rims, Gil Fernandez, George Preston, Andy Lacroix, and Bert Craven. Only Roy Ashton was missing from the lineup.

"Take a black felt-tip pen or whatever," said Vinnie, "and put knit caps and Hershey Bar mustaches on everybody."

Peggy used india ink and a crow-quill pen instead, for better control and to prevent feathering on the newsprint. Vinnie thanked her and took off for Calistoga after phoning Leonard Bontrager to make sure he was home.

Bontrager rented half of a ramshackle, white clapboard bungalow on Brannan Street. Scraggly grass and tall castor-bean plants tried to pass themselves off as a front garden. A big yellow dog heaved himself to his feet on the front porch as Vinnie came up the walk, barked a couple of token woofs, and lay down again.

Bontrager ushered Vinnie into his living room and invited him to take a seat on the sofa, upholstered in what looked like teddy-bear fur. The two other features in the room that caught his eye were a pink plaster plaque on the wall bearing the admonition BE YE PERFECT in blue letters ornamented with forget-me-nots, and three or four issues of *Penthouse* magazine on the coffee table.

"I . . . sublimate," said Bontrager with a grin. He sat down and studied the photographs Vinnie had laid out on the coffee table.

"Gosh, they all look alike!" Biting on a hangnail and frowning, he warily, tentatively, eliminated three. "If it has to be any of them, I suppose this would have to be the one," he concluded, pointing to Preston's picture, "but I can't say I'm rock-bottom sure of that one either. This other one's pretty close." The other one was Bert Craven. He declined to be more positive than that.

Vinnie thanked him and gathered up the photos. Bontrager accompanied him to the door. "Been thinking about your soul any? How is it today?"

"About like my Mercedes," said Vinnie, turning. "Needs a wash, but ticks over nicely."

Bontrager grinned. "You better take another look at John Three-sixteen. Oh—don't try to pet Fritz on your way out. He isn't mean but he don't like to be petted."

TWENTY-SEVEN

Holly Shelton was interested but less excited than Vinnie over Leonard Bontrager's narrowing the field to two suspects. She had seen too many cases of mistaken identity and heard too many witnesses swear that the same felon was five-nine and six-three, thin and fat, Anglo and Latino, long-haired and short-haired. Nor were a knit cap and a mustache much to go on. Nonetheless, she complimented Vinnie on his spadework, and especially his telling her all the details.

What Vinnie did *not* tell her was his plan for the evening that involved a coat hanger.

At 2:00 in the morning he and Peggy drove to Madrona Street in her little Ford Escort, the perfect car for the job, small, dusty, nondescript—and black. They parked by the curb between the second and third houses down from Adrienne's place. After checking to make sure nobody was on the street, Vinnie got out with his coat hanger. Peggy stayed at the wheel. She was to give a short toot on the horn only if she saw a pedestrian or a car slowing down while Vinnie was in plain sight.

All remained quiet. On rubber-soled shoes, Vinnie strolled as casually as he could toward Adrienne's driveway, where Preston's Cadillac was parked. He wished the place had dense shrubbery. He wished the night had been darker. The bright light of the waning moon was a problem. His shadow on the sidewalk was an india ink silhouette. However, a six-foot masonry brick wall on the other side of the driveway separated Adrienne's place from the house next door. Vinnie tiptoed up into the narrow space between the Cadillac and the wall. He waited there to make sure no lights went on in the house. It remained dark. That was good. If anyone came out, he would face two dreadful choices: Run away in the bright moonlight and hope he'd be mistaken for the Gingerbread Boy, or crawl under the car and, if caught, try to think up a logical reason for being there. (Got drunk? Scavenger hunt? Suddenly homeless?) The thought almost persuaded him he should go home and leave the matter up to Holly. Almost.

But the house remained dark, and Peggy was sitting back there waiting for him to be macho, so he straightened out the coat hanger into a single long wire, and moved to the door on the driver's side.

The rubber molding around the windows of an Eldorado, he found, was ridiculous—an inch thick overall, soft, with a good quarter of an inch showing between the top of the glass and the chrome frame. He bent the wire into a curve, inserted the hook under the rubber, pushed it down, and after two misses maneuvered the hook under the chrome lock-button, pulled up, and the door was unlocked. The whole operation took little more than twenty seconds. Child's play. He wondered for a moment why they even bother to put locks on a Cadillac.

He opened the door *and the ceiling light came on.* Terrified, he slid onto the front seat, and pulled the door closed enough to make the light go out. With buttocks clenched and sphincter contracted, he looked at the front of the house.

No porch light came on. After several moments his sphincter relaxed. He pushed the button on the glove compartment. Its door dropped open and a dim light went on inside.

A navy-blue knit cap lay on top of a smog-control certificate and a Thomas Guide to the roads and streets of Napa and Sonoma counties. Vinnie removed it and felt around the back of the glove compartment. His fingers brought out a wide and bushy false mustache.

Vinnie clenched his teeth in anger. He felt a momentary urge to forget about stealth and simply go pound on the goddamn door and try to beat that bastard Preston to a pulp when he opened it.

The rash urge gave way to better sense. He put the mustache and cap back into the glove compartment, and opened the door half an inch. He touched the lock button and slid out of the car fast because the ceiling light went on again. He pushed the door almost shut, and to avoid slamming it put his behind against it and pressed until it closed completely with a sharp click.

This time he hurried down the street to Peggy's car, got in, and tossed the coat hanger onto the backseat.

"How did it go?"

"Found 'em all right."

As Peggy gunned the motor into a U-turn, Adrienne's porch light went on. They didn't look back to see if anyone came out.

Holly would have some interesting news in the morning.

TWENTY-EIGHT

Damned if you aren't the eighth frigging wonder of the world!"

Holly Shelton's mouth curled upward in a smile as she looked at Vinnie across her desk, but her eyes squinted into a frown at the same time. "Do you realize I could arrest you for second-degree burglary?"

"Why? I didn't steal anything."

"You're guilty anyway according to Section Four fifty-nine of the California penal code."

"At least I got some hot information."

Holly's nostrils dilated as she took in a deep breath. "Vincent Letessier, you have interfered with an investigation, withheld evidence, and now you're a goddamn burglar! One more thing—just one—and you are in trouble."

"Don't I at least get an *A* for effort?"

"As a final grade, yes, but the semester's over, you understand?"

Vinnie saw it was wise to say nothing, and Holly cooled off.

"Meanwhile," she said, after a moment, "I've been collecting some hot information of my own."

"What is it?"

"Never mind. But together with what I've found out, and what you've just told me, I think I can get Judge Matsuoka to issue a search warrant for Adrienne Letessier's house and Preston's car."

"You going to tell him about my burglary?"

"Hell, no. I'll use Bontrager's probable identification as an excuse."

"This'll take a while, won't it?"

"Probably an hour or two."

"Can I wait here?"

"If you want to. Out in the lobby."

"On second thought, though," said Vinnie, "I'll run over to the County Building to see Lacroix. There's one last question we've forgotten to ask him: Where did he get the key to the fermentation room? He claims he picked the lock, but I don't believe him."

"Not bad, Sherlock. Think he'll tell you?"

"Does he have a choice?"

He didn't. The answer was that he got it from Nilla Toscana, who got it from Preston, who presumably wanted to get into Nilla's tank again, so to speak.

"So Preston was involved with that one too," said Holly, when she returned. "Busy guy. Thanks to you, of course, we can't nail him for it."

"What section of the penal code deals with stealing a body and sticking it in a fermentation tank?"

"I don't know, I'd have to look it up."

"Did you get the search warrant?"

"Yes, but Judge Matsuoka took one hell of a lot of convincing."

"When are you going to do it?"

"The search? Now. And I want you to come along. I want to keep this as low-key as I can. I'd rather go there with a civilian than another cop and I don't want to go alone."

"Are you going to deputize me?"

"This isn't Tombstone, Arizona, Letessier. I can't just pin a badge on you. You have to go through basic training to be a deputy sheriff."

"Oh."

"What I *am* going to do is 'summon you to my aid,' as it says in section eight thirty-six(b), but only for the sole purpose of this search. You'll have the powers of a legitimate peace officer till it's over."

"Swell, but why do I need any powers?"

"In case there's a brouhaha. I'm only five-three and you're, what? Six-four?"

"Three."

"Whatever. By the way, I overheard your uncle calling me Barbie Doll that time."

"I warned him about that. Anyway, I hope there *is* a brouhaha. I'd love to get my hands on Preston if he really is the one."

"Failing that, I can always fall back on my Smith and Wesson Thirty-eight. Let's go."

The two of them strolled up Adrienne's front walk as casually as they could, Vinnie with his hands in his pockets. They saw George Preston looking at them from the picture window but he quickly disappeared from view.

"Nice barrel cactus," said Holly. She rang the doorbell.

Adrienne, wide-eyed, opened the door.

"Good morning, Mrs. Letessier. As you know, I'm investigating the murder of Francis Letessier, and I have a search warrant for these premises. That includes the

Cadillac Eldorado in the driveway." She handed it to Adrienne. "May I come in?"

Adrienne stared at the paper for half a minute, but clearly was not reading it. When she finally looked up, her eyes were furious and she was breathing heavily.

"This is an insult! An outrage! I'll sue! I'll sue the county for this!"

"Nobody's been arrested yet."

"And what the hell is *he* doing here?"

"You might say I drafted him, so he's a peace officer for the time being. May we come in now? Let's keep this as quiet as possible."

Adrienne stepped back and swung the door open, bowing and sweeping her arm in mock welcome.

"It appears we have *guests,* George," she said. Preston, wearing a fishing vest bulging at the pockets, joined the group in the living room.

"I'll ask you two to remain here while I do the search," said Holly. "Vincent, stay here and keep an eye on them. Make sure they don't leave the room."

"An *eye?*" said Adrienne, as Holly went off to begin her search. "A *private* eye? Do you mind if I smoke— *private eye?*"

"They're your lungs."

Both Adrienne and Preston lit cigarettes. Preston blew out a cloud of smoke and glowered through it at Vinnie. "I'm going to get you for this, Letessier!"

"I doubt it. I'm facing you this time. But I hope you try, Preston."

There was no more conversation. Words could hardly have penetrated the anger and hatred that hung in the air like a poisonous gas.

Vinnie, with no book to read, perused Adrienne instead. She was again wearing her red blouse and white shorts, and her tan was deeper than ever. She stood with her legs apart, defiant, gorgeous, and smoldering. Vinnie thought of John Wayne's great line to Susan Hayward when he played Genghis Khan: "Yo're lovely in yore wrath."

But all good things must come to an end. When Holly returned to the living room she carried a plastic evidence bag, a book, and a can of drain opener.

"I'll need your car keys now, Mr. Preston."

Preston, grim, eyes flashing, flung them at her feet. She picked them up and went outside. She came back with another evidence bag containing a knit cap and false mustache.

"What do you think that proves?" said Preston.

"Nothing, necessarily, but a witness believes you wore these on the night of the murder."

"Oh, yeah? What witness?"

"I also talked to the vet who treats the horses at Bob Simmons's ranch in the Alexander Valley, where I know you've worked. He was missing a few gelatin capsules out of his kit, but thought nothing about it. I found the chemical under the kitchen sink, and this—" Holly held up a copy of *The Anarchist Cookbook*—"in your room, with passages marked. You did okay in chemistry in your one semester at UC Davis—but this was not very smart, Mr. Preston."

"Well, you listen to me, Tootsie. I haven't done a damn thing, and all you've got there is a bunch of meaningless knickknacks."

"It's enough to go on."

"Bull. Any of your cop friends'll tell you this is nothing but circumstantial evidence and flimsy at that."

"Right. Defense lawyers say that all the time, but circumstantial evidence is usually the only kind there is, unless people see the defendant standing over the body with a smoking gun. Among other charges, Mr. Preston, I'm arresting you on suspicion of first-degree murder."

Holly read him his Miranda rights from a card and detached a pair of handcuffs from her belt. "Put these on Mr. Preston, Vincent—hands behind the back."

189

"That son of a bitch is not going to touch me!"

Adrienne stepped forward, hands on hips. "What the hell's the idea anyway? You want the neighbors to see him walk out of my house in *handcuffs?*"

"It's required procedure, Ms. Letessier."

"I don't give a shit! This isn't a goddamn TV show!"

"Forget it, Adrienne! I'm not going anywhere!"

"Calm down, Mr. Preston! It'll go better for you if you cooperate."

"I said I'm not going anywhere!"

From a pocket of his fishing vest, Preston drew out a glass bottle containing perhaps a quarter of a pint of almost colorless liquid.

"This is nitro!" he snarled. "And it isn't for my heart, Tootsie!"

Holly drew her pistol.

Preston was not intimidated. "Drop that or I'll blow up the whole fucking place! Car keys, Detective Shelton." He held out his left hand.

She tossed them at his feet. He was careful enough to pick them up without taking his eyes off her.

"Gun on the floor!"

Holly wavered. Preston lifted the bottle high over his head.

"Now! Slow!"

Holly stooped and laid the revolver on the tiles.

"Kick it over here!"

Holly drew her foot back.

"No, Holly!" exclaimed Vinnie. "Let him throw it!"

"Vincent!"

"Pick up your gun, Holly."

"Touch that gun and everybody's dead!" said Preston, gritting his teeth.

"George!" Adrienne cried out. "What about me?"

He laughed a bitter laugh. "You? You were going to dump me!"

"No, George! I swear to God!"

"After the favor I did you! You hated him, and so did I!"

"*Favor!* You mean Francis? I didn't *hate* him! You killed Francis as a *favor?* Acing me out of five thousand a month was a *favor?*"

"It was, to Nilla," said Vinnie.

"Oh yes! Nilla!" said Adrienne. "I know you're still sniffing around her!"

"Why not? She cut me in on the Triskelion deal—and she's a better lay than *you* ever were, you egotistical bitch!"

Adrienne was enraged. "*She's* the one you did the *favor* for!"

"Screw this! Kick that gun over here or I throw the nitro!"

"Go ahead, George," said Vinnie.

"You think I won't?"

"I don't know. Maybe."

"Vincent, *will you let me handle this!*" said Holly.

Vinnie picked up the revolver and aimed it at Preston. "Boy, does this ever feel good! I've been hoping for this moment, Preston—but first I'm going to count to five. One."

Holly looked at him, terrified. "Vincent, are you crazy?"

"Two."

"You're going with me!" said Preston.

"Three."

"*For God's sake!*" Adrienne shouted. "*Both of you!*"

"Four."

Before Vinnie could say *five,* Preston, wild-eyed, gave an anguished yell and slammed the bottle onto the tiles as the two women screamed.

Glass shattered but there was no explosion.

Preston gaped at the oily slick on the floor. Holly and Adrienne stood frozen with their hands over their mouths.

Vinnie handed the cuffs to Holly. "Here, you do it. I'll hold the gun."

Preston was stupefied. He made no move to stop Holly from handcuffing him, and leading him out to the sheriff's department car.

Judge Matsuoka ordered Preston held without bail.

Back at her desk, Holly asked Vinnie with a grin, "How did you know that wasn't nitroglycerin?"

"Oh, but it was!"

"It *was?* And you let him *throw* it?"

"Sure."

"You risked all of our lives?"

"No. I dated a girl at UCLA whose father was an executive at the Hercules Powder Company. He said he always got a laugh out of those TV scenes like the one with Preston. Regardless of what everybody thinks, he said you can't detonate nitro that way. He wished people could see what goes on at Hercules—nitroglycerin pouring out of a pipe and dropping six feet into a basin. The main precaution they take is having the workers in that room wear lead-soled shoes."

Holly leaned back in her chair. "Vincent, as far as I can tell, you have about as much talent for detective work as Porky Pig—but my god, do you ever cash in on serendipity and blind-ass luck!"

Vinnie was stung. "I thought I did a hell of a job!"

"Get out of here. Go back to your winery. No, go to Las Vegas and play roulette. Put all your chips on thirty-three. You'll make a fortune."

"Don't I even get a medal or something?" he said, rising.

"You'll get the thanks of your grateful government." She smiled at him. "And my thanks. Yes, Vincent, you did a hell of a job."

The phone rang. She picked it up. "Sheriff's investigations, Holly Shelton speaking, may I help you, please?"

Vinnie walked out. With a new appreciation for female detectives.

TWENTY-NINE

For the remainder of October, nature held its breath, and its rain. The dry weather held.

By the first week of November most of the tourists were long gone, but a coterie of diehards—mostly from Southern California, where there would be no autumn at all if the ginkgo trees didn't turn yellow—hung on. They were ecstatic to see, here and there, vineyards so aflame in red leaves that it looked like Vermont. The vintners who owned those vines were not ecstatic, but they smiled at the gushing tourists anyway—and didn't tell them that red leaves in a cabernet vineyard are a sign of incurable leaf roll virus, and that the afflicted vines will produce 10 percent less for the rest of their lives.

Château Letessier escaped that version of beauty, but

faced a crucial decision. "It's up to you guys," said Gil Fernandez. "Do we harvest the gewürztraminer now, at thirty-seven percent, or hang on for another week and hope it doesn't rain?"

"What do you think, Dik?" said Vinnie.

"What do you think, Vinnie?" he answered with a grin.

"What do you think, Gil?" said Vinnie.

"It isn't my money—so sure, I'd say let's shoot the works."

"Okay with you, Dik?"

"Okay with me."

They crossed their fingers and won. They harvested the gewürztraminer on the tenth of November at 40 percent, Fernandez nursed a magnificent wine through the bottling process, and they waited for the money to roll in on Corpus Christi Day.

In the meantime, the partners threw an Armenian picnic to celebrate. All the employees of the winery came, including the women who pasted labels on bottles; and Dikran's brothers were all there—Krikor, Aram, and Mourad. Satenig Arshagouni prepared all the food herself: marinated leg of lamb, dolmas wrapped in grape leaves from the gewürztraminer vineyard, tabbouleh, rice with mushrooms, and baklava. Vinnie dug out ten bottles of the prized 1974 Point Zéro cabernet sauvignon, after a few glasses of which Satenig sang "Groonk" again. She wavered a trifle off-key, but only Dikran noticed and he didn't care.

Vinnie had something on his mind. Sitting with Dik at the far end of the picnic table, he cleared his throat and said, "Dik, you know good wine and I know good wine, but who around here knows the most about making wine—and running a winery?"

Dik reflected a moment. "Gil Fernandez."

"Right. So wouldn't it be smart if we made him a partner?"

196

"Come to think of it, yes. Great idea. If he ever left, we'd be up Bitter Creek without a paddle."

"Then what do you say we do it?"

They called him over and did it—and three minutes later saw Holly throwing her arms around him and patting his back.

Vinnie and Dik watched them with delight. Dik lifted his glass and said, "She may be a homicide detective, but he'll lay down the law tonight!"

"That one has whiskers on it!" said Vinnie, and punched him in the shoulder.

Another important event had occurred the day before: Andy Lacroix lost his seat on the county Board of Supervisors by a sizable margin. His erstwhile supporters felt he had betrayed them by his new opposition to development, and 40 percent of the electorate never liked him in the first place. Lacroix reopened his radio and electronics store.

"He and Preston were quite a pair, weren't they?" said Dik. "Too damn clever for their own good."

"There's an old Armenian proverb . . ." Vinnie began.

Dik laughed. *"You* are quoting old Armenian *proverbs?"*

"There's an old Armenian proverb—which I'm sure your grandfather Khosrove remembers: 'The fox's last hole is the furrier's shop.' "

GAYLORD RG